the undertow

PETER CORRIS is known as the 'godfather' of Australian crime fiction through his Cliff Hardy detective stories. He has written in many other areas, including a co-authored autobiography of the late Professor Fred Hollows, a history of boxing in Australia, spy novels, historical novels and a collection of short stories revolving around the game of golf (see www.petercorris.net). He is married to writer Jean Bedford and lives in Sydney. They have three daughters.

PETER CORRIS

the undertow

A CLIFF HARDY NOVEL

ALLEN&UNWIN

Thanks to Jean Bedford and Jo Jarrah

First published in 2006

Allen & Unwin
83 Alexander Street
Crows Nest NSW 2065
Australia
Phone: (61 2) 8425 0100
Fax: (61 2) 9906 2218
Email: info@allenandunwin.com
Web: www.allenandunwin.com

National Library of Australia
Cataloguing-in-Publication entry:

Corris, Peter, 1942– .
  The Undertow: a Cliff Hardy novel.

  ISBN 978 1 74114 748 3.

  ISBN 1 74114 748 4.

  1. Hardy, Cliff (Fictitious character) – Fiction.
  2. Private investigators – New South Wales – Sydney –
  Fiction. I. Title.

A823.3

Set in 12/14 pt Adobe Garamond by Midland Typesetters, Australia
Printed in Australia by McPherson's Printing Group

10 9 8 7 6 5 4 3 2 1

For Tom Kelly

part one

1

'It's a long time ago, Frank,' I said.

Frank Parker stroked his grey stubble as if to indicate the passage of time. 'Twenty-three years. That's not so long. Seems like yesterday the way time flies now.'

I knew what he meant. When I was a kid the summer school holidays stretched forever, and in winter it seemed as if summer and surfing would never come. I couldn't afford a wetsuit and had to wait at least until late September to hit the water. Now the years dropped away like the calendar leaves in an old Warner Brothers movie. Still, twenty years was a long time to go back digging up an old murder case.

Frank, retired from the police force as a deputy commissioner, and a long time friend married to Hilde, my former tenant and nothing more than a close friend, had asked me to visit him to talk something over. I was surprised to find that Hilde was away for the day attending a social work conference in the Blue Mountains. Frank could have had me over anytime and it seemed that he'd deliberately picked a day when Hilde wasn't there.

'It's niggled at me every day since,' Frank said, working on his second stubbie since I arrived. Two in an hour was

3

fast work for Frank. After some pleasantries and with the first of our beers in hand, he'd said he wanted me to take a look at the Gregory Heysen case. Heysen was a doctor who'd been convicted of hiring a hit man to kill his partner in their Darlinghurst practice.

'I remember the name, but I forget the details, if I ever knew them,' I said. 'You'd better tell me why it's got you so worried. And why do I get the feeling you didn't want Hilde around while we talked about this?'

Frank sighed and looked his age, which was just the other side of sixty. He played tennis, swam, didn't smoke, was a light drinker and both his parents had lived into their nineties. He'd always looked twenty years younger than his age but not now. 'Smart bastard, aren't you?' he said.

I shrugged, took a swig on the Stella. 'I can usually spot the obvious.'

'Okay. It's like this. I was one of the team investigating the murder of Peter Bellamy. It was one of the biggest hands-on jobs I'd had since getting out of uniform. I shouldn't have been anywhere near it.'

'Why?'

'I'd had an affair with Catherine. This was before I met Hilde.'

'Catherine?'

'Catherine Beddoes, Heysen's wife. It went on for a little while after she married Heysen. I didn't know that. She didn't tell me she was married. Then she did and I ended it.'

'Jesus, Frank.'

'I know, I know. I should've declared a conflict of interest and butted out.'

'Why didn't you?'

Frank drained his stubbie and looked almost angry and upset enough to throw it into the pool. We were sitting in the back yard of his Paddington terrace. He'd bought it when you could buy houses in Paddo without needing a six figure income. He still had some mortgage, he'd told me, but with lots of equity at current prices. He'd been able to renovate and put the pool in with part of his super.

'I was ambitious, wanted to make a step up. I didn't know that there'd be a clearing out of the corrupt bastards above me and that my promotion would be . . . accelerated anyway. The Heysen case was high profile and tricky. We got a break and cracked it. Kudos all around.'

'But?'

'I had some doubts. You mostly do except when it's open and shut. Which it usually is, you know—domestic, financial, sexual . . .'

I nodded.

'Bellamy and Heysen seemed to get on well. They'd graduated from Sydney uni at much the same time, done locums, knocked around, borrowed the dough to set up the practice and were doing okay. They bulk-billed, put in the hours, worked their arses off. Made house calls, would you believe?'

'Dinosaur stuff.'

'Right. They both lived more or less locally—Bellamy in Darlinghurst, Heysen in Earlwood.'

'That's not local.'

'Close enough. A big difference between them emerged—Bellamy was gay, Heysen was straight, very straight. Hadn't known about Bellamy's orientation. After a while, Bellamy started to actively attract HIV positives and AIDS cases to the practice and Heysen didn't like it.'

'Uh oh.'

'Yeah. Bad vibes. Bellamy accuses Heysen of homo-phobia, spreads the word. Heysen's client list starts to slip. The two can hardly bear to lay eyes on each other so they have to do something. Heysen offers to buy Bellamy out but Bellamy isn't interested. Turns out Heysen hasn't got the money anyway. In fact, having recently got married, bought a house and with a child and a demanding wife, he's asset-rich but cash-poor. All this talking's making my throat dry. I'm having another beer. You?'

'Sure.'

Frank went inside and I got up and dipped my hand in the pool. It was late March and the water was still at a comfortable temperature. Made me wish I had a pool, but everything in Frank's behaviour showed that he had problems that I was sure I didn't want.

Frank came back with the beers and started talking before he sat down. 'Then it gets sleazy. Bellamy's out cruising and he gets stabbed to death. We work it and it looks like a standard homosexual killing—wrong move made at the wrong time to the wrong person, you know. Bellamy seemed to be popular and he'd become a spokesman for the gays and we were anxious not to be branded as homophobic and all that, so we did the legwork. Talked to everyone, probed the backgrounds and fore-grounds. All we came up with was the animosity between the two of them, but Heysen seemed to be above suspicion. He couldn't afford to buy his partner out, but he wasn't exactly on the breadline. Plus . . .' Frank took a long pull on his stubbie, 'his wife's family had some money.

'The pressure came on to crack it and we got a break. An informant of mine steered us to Rafael Padrone, a low-lifer who's got terminal cancer. Heysen was treating him. Under the sort of pressure we could apply back then, Padrone says Heysen hired him to kill Bellamy and paid him twenty grand. Padrone's got all the details right, including those little things we held back. He's also got fifteen thousand bucks stashed and Heysen can't account for twenty thousand that should have been in the practice's account and isn't. And Padrone hasn't had a bill for his treatments.'

'Pretty circumstantial.'

'Yeah, but compelling enough for the DPP. Heysen was an arrogant prick and made a terrible impression in interviews, not to mention his trial. Padrone had pleaded guilty and everything he'd said was on video. He was sentenced to fourteen years and was dead in six months. Heysen got fourteen as well, for conspiracy to commit murder. QED. You must remember this.'

I thought about it. One thing I knew for sure was that Frank had never mentioned it to me, and we'd discussed most of our more interesting cases over the years. Sydney throws up murders and conspiracies, trials and appeals, judgements and sentences every year and they tend to blend together. I had only the vaguest recollection of the name Heysen, and then probably because I quite liked some of Hans Heysen's paintings and had a print of one in my house. I shook my head. 'Barely a glimmer of it,' I said. 'What were your doubts about?'

'It was all a bit too neat. Virtually a dying confession. An obvious suspect. Pressure for closure. Everything.'

'But you went along.'

'It was out of my hands. I gave my evidence straight. Heysen's lawyer was competent—he's dead too, by the way—and he grilled me good, but I didn't get any opportunity to express doubts and they had no solid foundation anyway. Fuck it, Padrone was a waste of space and Heysen treated me like shit. He looked and sounded guilty.'

'The human element.'

'Exactly. Anyway, Heysen went to gaol. Had a hard time for a while, the way all educated people do, but he settled down and became a model prisoner. He did medical work above and beyond the call of duty. Came up for parole after twelve years, made a bad impression on the board and got knocked back. Came up again two years later and was found dead in his cell before the hearing. Natural causes, brain haemorrhage brought on by stress. He had high blood pressure.'

'Well, it's an interesting story, Frank, but I can't see why you want it looked into now. I mean, all the parties are dead.'

'Not quite.'

'No?'

'There's me and Catherine Heysen and her son, William. Catherine got in touch with me a week or so ago. She says her son's on the skids. She kept what had happened to her husband from him for most of his life but he found out not long back. She thought he was old enough to handle it, but he wasn't, apparently. It rocked him. He started to drink, use drugs, hang out with losers.'

'That's tough on her, but what's it got to do with you?'

The lines and grooves in Frank's face, the marks of character, experience and physical fitness, took on an eroded, desiccated look. 'Catherine took up with Heysen while she was still on with me and kept seeing me for a while, as I said. She says William is my son.'

2

It's not something that's easy to explain to those who haven't been through it. Frank knew that some time back I'd discovered that I had a daughter I hadn't known existed. My then wife, Cyn, had concealed her pregnancy from me at the time of our acrimonious breakup and had had the child adopted. After a lot of angst, it worked out okay between the daughter, Megan, and me and there was some sort of deathbed reconciliation between Cyn and Megan and Cyn's daughter by her second marriage. It doesn't always turn out so well.

'It's bloody difficult,' Frank said. 'I don't know whether Catherine's telling the truth and I can't let Hilde find out about it, one way or the other, just now.'

'Why not? Hilde knows you weren't a virgin before you met her. How could you be? You were what, in your late thirties?'

'She's menopausal, Cliff—very up and down. And Peter's away somewhere in fucking South America. We hear from him once in a blue moon. He makes noises about staying there. Hilde's learning Spanish and not liking it. South America's where a lot of the Nazis went and you

9

know what she thinks about them. I can't hit her with this now. Catherine's sort of . . . pressuring me.'

Peter was the Parkers' son—what we atheists called my anti-godson as a joke. After doing a science degree, he worked for Greenpeace in various parts of the world and was seldom in Australia. He was a risk-taker and Hilde worried about him constantly. A tough survivor herself, with aunts, uncles and cousins swept away in the Holocaust, she had a need to rebuild a family and Peter wasn't helping. But Frank's hesitation suggested another level of trouble.

'Tell me about Catherine.'

'She's convinced that Heysen wasn't guilty. She wants me to prove it. She thinks that if William learns that his father wasn't a convicted murderer but a respected doctor, he'll change his ways. Go back to being the good kid he was before he found out.'

'That's not what I meant, Frank, and you know it.'

'Yeah, yeah. She's a good deal younger than me. She's persuasive and very attractive. I can't see her again, can't have anything to do with her directly. That's why I'm asking you to help me.'

'What about the boy?'

'Christ, I don't know. She could be lying but she says a DNA test'd prove it. I can't go through that. This thing's like an undertow, Cliff. It's pulling me down.'

Of course I agreed to do what I could. Frank had sat at his computer sometime and written down everything he could remember about the Heysen case—names, places and dates. He gave me the printout amounting to over fifty pages. An almost eidetic memory had been one of his strengths as a detective, and when he quoted some of the people involved I was prepared to believe it was near to word-for-word accurate.

Frank looked at his watch and I took the hint. I folded the dossier and watched him take money from his wallet.

'Frank.'

'We've got a joint account. I can't give you a cheque.'

'I'm not taking your money.'

'You fucking are. I want you full-time on this and fair dinkum. It could get expensive. Some of these people have probably scattered. Here.'

He handed me ten one hundred dollar notes. 'Won't Hilde notice you're down a bit?'

'Let me worry about that. Cliff, I hate doing this without her knowing—'

'Me, too.'

'But I've got no choice. I can't really help you either. I guess you could ring me once or twice if you need to, and visit, but Hilde'd get suspicious if it was more often. Shit, I hate this.'

'It's okay. I'll play it your way, but we have to agree on one thing—if for some reason it becomes necessary for Hilde to learn everything about it, that's the way it'll have to be.'

'You're a cunning bastard, Cliff.'

'A survivor. Agreed?'

'Yes.'

We shook hands, something we never usually did. It marked how different this meeting had been from all the others and I hoped it didn't mean any kind of change for the worse.

Frank seemed to sense something similar, and he grinned and did a mock shape-up. 'I feel better now that I know you're helping, mate.'

I nodded. He collected the empties and stowed them carefully in the recycle bin. I wondered if Hilde knew how many beers had been on hand and would notice how many had been drunk. Or would Frank have that covered somehow? A long-time deceiver myself, the standard line came to my mind: *Oh, what a tangled web we weave . . .*

We walked past the pool to the gate. 'Any tips, Frank?'

'I thought you said you could spot the obvious.'

'Start with Catherine.'

'Right,' he said.

I felt very uneasy as I drove home. Frank Parker was one of the steadiest, most composed men I'd ever known and it shook me to see him so rattled. It was understandable. There'd recently been a case involving a high profile public person in a similar situation. It had turned out strangely and the letters page of the papers had been full of contradictory opinions on adoption, DNA testing, the rights of adults and children when paternity was in doubt or contested. No such strong media light would be shone on Frank's dilemma, but the pressures on all parties were the same. Except for Dr Gregory Heysen—dead while still in prison, possibly for a crime he didn't commit.

3

For the first time in years, I had a live-in partner, even if only temporarily. I'd been in a casual relationship with Lily Truscott for some time. We'd spend a night together now and then, sometimes at her place, sometimes at mine, and there'd be weeks when we didn't see each other at all. Lily had been editor of the *Australian Financial Review*, then a feature writer and now she was freelancing. Her house was in Greenwich and one of Sydney's wild storms brought a huge tree down on top of it. The house lost its roof and several exterior and interior walls. Driving rain and wind just about demolished it. Lily moved in with me while her place was being rebuilt. She was fully insured, but the company dragged out the process the way they do, and the rebuilding was slowed down by council obstructions and the usual problems with tradesmen, so that Lily's stay was stretching out.

It was working well, though. Lily was interstate often, chasing stories, and I never knew quite where I'd be from one day to the next. No expectations on either side. We were both fond of a drink, keen on exercise, undiscriminating about food. Like me, Lily preferred Dylan to Dvorak and le Carré to Henry James, Spielberg to Bergman. We talked about our jobs when we were together; I learned a bit about insider trading and unions in the Pilbara, and she picked up stuff on surveillance and tracing missing persons.

Lily was coming down the stairs when I arrived home from the meeting with Frank. She has shoulder-length dark-blonde hair with a bit of grey and her face is smoother than it ought to be given some of the things she's been through. She was wearing a long white T-shirt and black pants and looked good, the way a woman who stands 180 centimetres and weighs about 70 kilos does.

'I need broadband,' she said. 'That fucking dial-up's too slow.'

'It's fast enough for me.'

Lily leased a state-of-the-art laptop after she lost everything in her house, but my basic dial-up arrangement for the Web didn't suit her. She worked in the spare room where my clunking old Mac now sat shamefacedly apart from her gleaming model.

'Yeah, your computer skills are definitely twentieth century—at best. When my place is up and running, I'm going to have wall-to-wall 2010 everything. Is that a bottle you've got there?'

She came down the stairs and gave me a hug and we opened the bottle of red and sat out the back where the autumn sun had just about retreated. The bricks I'd laid— very inexpertly, after chopping up ancient concrete back when Cyn and I bought the place—were still warm. Leaves were falling from the shrubs and drifting in from outside and I made a mental note to sweep them up. Sometime.

'What's on your plate, Lil?'

'The multifunction polis. Remember that?'

'Vaguely.'

'Right, you and everyone else. I'm off to Adelaide tomorrow to look into how it's going. You?'

Lily had met Frank and Hilde a few times, liked them, and knew how close we were. I told her about Frank's problem as we worked through the Merlot.

'Tricky,' she said.

I sneezed; the drifting leaves activated a mild allergy of some kind. I pulled a tissue from my pocket and Frank's money came out with it.

'Nice,' she said.

I blew my nose. 'Yeah—hidden from Hilde. Frank's cut up about it.'

'D'you think he's . . . in love with this Catherine?'

'No, but you know what men're like.'

'Don't I just? Would you go off me, Cliff? If I went into mood swings and hot flushes?'

'Mood swings you've already got. I don't know if hot flushes'd bother me.'

'We'll have to wait and see, won't we?'

I said, 'I read somewhere about DNA tests. Apparently one in four shows that your poppa ain't your poppa. Remember the song?'

'No, you're older than me, remember.'

'That's right. Any tips on handling this, Lil? I read the other day that males are better at asking how things work and females are better at human relationships.'

'Yeah—watch yourself with Catherine thingo. If she's got to old Frankie, she could get to you.'

I phoned the late Dr Heysen's widow in the morning while Lily was waiting for her cab to the airport. I told Catherine Heysen that Frank Parker had enlisted my help and she agreed to meet me at her place in Earlwood at 11 am. Her voice was the kind they classify as educated Australian. Tells you nothing, because there are various ways of acquiring it.

'You old charmer, you,' Lily said as I put the phone down.

'Less of the old. What's that supposed to mean?'

'I often wonder, after people hear you on the phone, all mild-mannered and persuasive, what they think when they get a look at you.'

'You mean the busted nose and the scar tissue?'

'And other things.'

'I'll tell you—they think, that bloke's been through a bit and maybe he'll go through a bit more for me. Also, they notice the good teeth.'

'Capped.'

'A touch of vanity for reassurance.'

The taxi horn sounded in the street and I carried Lily's bag out. A brief hug and kiss and then she was off. I didn't ask when she'd be back, as she never asked me—that wasn't the deal. She looked very good in her suit and heels and I knew that I'd soon be missing her taking the mickey out of me and making love with energy and humour.

I spent the next hour or so working through Frank's file and putting names, addresses and phone numbers in my notebook. The case had a formidable cast of characters, including detectives still serving and no longer serving, witnesses to disagreements between Heysen and Bellamy, associates of Rafael Padrone and experts of various kinds. Heysen's barrister was dead, as Frank had said, and so was the trial judge, but Heysen's solicitor and the prosecutor were still alive. Their details went into the notebook, although Frank cautioned that the addresses and phone numbers might be out of date.

There was a detailed description of the crime scene; reconstructions, as best Frank could remember them, of interviews with Heysen and others; and his recollection of how the Heysen finances stood. There'd been a substantial mortgage on the Earlwood house but Catherine Heysen was still there now, despite the couple's income dropping to zero. Interesting. The son, William, had been an infant at the time of the trial and he barely rated a mention. Heysen had been struck off the medical register after his conviction and his appeal had been refused. Not surprising. A number of Bellamy's patients and lovers had been interviewed. Frank had some of the names but no further details and, given the AIDS epidemic at the time, it was problematic how many would still be around.

Apart from it involving a close friend, it was the kind of case that interested me. Also the kind you had to work hard at to get a result. A money-spinner, but I didn't want to bleed Frank.

The Heysen house was a big, sprawling affair on a corner block overlooking the Cooks River and a stretch of green beyond that. The water view wouldn't have been an asset in days gone by when the Cooks River was more or less a sewer cum toxic waste dump, but it'll become more acceptable as the river gets rehabilitated. Long way to go. The government is said to have promised the money, but nothing much seems to be happening. With half a million people living along the river's banks, I suppose cleaning it is a big ask. There were more apartment blocks in the locality than freestanding houses.

I parked in the street and looked the place over more closely. It was far too big for a woman and a child as things must have stood when Dr Heysen went inside. Probably they'd planned a large family. Still, I wondered why she hadn't traded it in on something more manageable.

I could see a large garden in front and down the side, through an electronically controlled gate, a wide driveway. There was enough grass to keep a Victa busy for an hour or so. The corner block was deep, so there was probably more garden and grass at the back. Quite a few tall trees graced the scene, no doubt harbouring birds and cicadas, but also likely to drop leaves into the guttering. Okay for the doc who could afford to hire help, but what about the widow?

Frank's notes on her were minimal, as if he couldn't bear to think about her too much. She was forty-six now and had been a dental nurse before her marriage to Heysen at age twenty-two. Her father had been a champion cricketer and an executive in a large sporting goods firm. I had no information on her mother or on whether either of her parents was still alive. Given her age it was more than possible. Then again, if they'd died asset-rich, maybe she'd inherited the means to keep this big joint going.

I was respectably turned out in dark slacks, a blazer and a blue business shirt. No tie; I draw the line at ties. I opened the gate and tramped up the steep, central path to a set of steps leading to a wide porch at the front of the house, which had a white stucco finish. The condition of that kind of surface can tell you something, and in this case it told me that the house was well-maintained. No serious flaking. A security screen covered the solid front door. I rang the bell and waited. In a place this size, if she was having her morning tea out the back, it could take a while to get to the front door. Might not even hear the bell.

The door opened and she stood there in the late morning light. Even with my vision impeded by the screen, I could see why Frank was feeling the undertow: Catherine Heysen was one of the most beautiful women I'd ever seen.

'Mr Hardy?'

'Yes.'

She unlocked the security screen. 'Please come in.'

She stepped aside to let me in and then moved swiftly ahead of me down the passage. The quick glimpse I'd caught of her was a total surprise. She had very dark hair and eyes and an olive complexion. In a black dress with a couple of fine gold chains around her neck, she looked as Mediterranean as the Isle of Capri. She was medium tall and strongly built and her walk was stately.

I followed her past several rooms off the passage to left and right and through a well-appointed kitchen to a conservatory equipped with cane chairs and a low, glass-topped table. Outside the air was cool and getting cooler as a southerly gained strength, but this space had trapped the weakening sunlight and it was warm. Her gesture for me to sit was balletic, but natural.

'Please sit down, Mr Hardy. I've made some coffee. I'm sure you'd like some after being out in that wind.'

I thanked her and took one of the comfortably padded chairs. The walls were mostly glass and a skylight took up a good part of the roof. There were a couple of pot stands with plants sprouting, and a cabinet with some porcelain pieces displayed. The parquet floor was mostly covered by an expensive-looking rug in muted colours—Greek,

Turkish, Moroccan? I wouldn't know. The exposed parts of
the floor were dust free.

She came back with the coffee things on a tray. She laid
them out expertly but without fuss and sat opposite me. My
cup was two-thirds full and the cream and sugar were to
hand. I took a sip and it was the kind of coffee you didn't
need to do anything to. She added a little cream to her cup
and raised it to her full lips. Every move she made was
potentially entrancing, and I had to struggle not to watch
her for the sheer pleasure of it.

'I knew Frank would help me,' she said, 'so it didn't
surprise me when you rang. I understand why he wants to
stay . . . at arm's length.'

Do you? I wondered. I doubted it, but her attitude was
certainly helpful at this point. I nodded and drank some
more of the excellent coffee. Like a psychoanalyst, a private
detective likes to hear people talk. You can learn a lot about
them that way, not necessarily from what they're saying.

'I hope you're not focusing on the matter of the
paternity of my son.'

'For the moment, I'm taking that as given, with reser-
vations. What I'm most interested in is why you're so
convinced that your husband wasn't guilty of arranging
Dr Bellamy's death.'

'Thank God for someone with directness as well as
subtlety.'

I wasn't going to let her snow me like that. 'Of course,
there are lots of other questions.'

'Such as?'

'You might find some of them offensive. Let's pursue
the matter I raised while we're still being polite.'

I drained my cup and she took another sip before

pushing the pot towards me. 'I don't agree. Let's deal with the offensive questions first, and then see whether we can still . . . communicate.'

'Okay. I'm wondering why and how you keep living here. There must be six or seven bedrooms. One for every night of the week.'

It came out more rudely than I'd intended, but something about her gracious control was getting under my skin. She didn't blink an eye, or twitch or fiddle with her coffee cup.

'Did Frank have anything to say about this?'

'No. He said you had some money. He implied not a lot.'

'That's so. I struggled for twelve years to keep the house because I couldn't believe my husband was guilty and I was sure something would turn up and he'd be released. I wanted the house to be here for him. I'd done some part-time work as a photographic model before I was married and I went back to it full-time, here and overseas. I hated it, but it paid well. I was able to keep the house and educate William. Also to pay my husband's life insurance premiums. When he died there was a lot of money suddenly.'

'I see. And why stay after he died?'

She sighed. 'Laziness, inertia. The thought of moving horrifies me. And the space wasn't as wasted as you seem to think. William had a bedroom and a . . . study. I dabbled in photography and painting. One of the rooms is a studio and one a darkroom. Are you satisfied?'

It sounded convincing, if also a bit rehearsed. But maybe she was one of those people who run over the story of their own lives in their heads and can trot it out pat. For the moment, she'd faced me down and it was my turn to be gracious.

'I'm sorry. That's interesting and all a credit to you, I'd say.'

'Thank you.'

'Could you give me a photograph of William?'

She smiled her Madonna smile. 'Of course. So you can see if he looks like Frank?'

'No, so I'll know him when and if I meet him.'

Something about her reaction to what I said—a blink, a small nod, a tightening of her mouth—told me a lot. Despite her earlier remark, she was as concerned about the boy, perhaps his whereabouts, as about clearing her husband's name. Two sides of the same coin, although she wasn't yet prepared to admit it. To be honest, it was my main interest, but I had to step carefully.

'You seem to be confident of doing that,' she said.

'Mrs Heysen,' I said, 'if you're not confident at this stage of an investigation you're in the wrong business.'

She nodded, stood and walked out of the room. I poured myself some more coffee. It was cool but so good it didn't matter. She came back and put a photograph down on the table, keeping another in her hand. 'This is William,' she said.

A young man with a shapely, sculptured nose, face and jaw was grinning into the camera. He had a mop of dark hair and his grin was slightly lopsided. It took a lot of imagination to see him as a younger version of long-headed Frank Parker. She noticed my reaction and passed me the other photo.

'And this is my husband just before he went to prison.'

The man in the suit with a serious expression was

stocky and moon-faced. I looked up at her as she stood regally above me.

'I wanted to be married and to have children and Frank . . . didn't,' she said. 'William and Frank are nothing alike, are they?'

'No,' I said. 'Your son looks like you, which is his good fortune.'

'Thank you.' She resumed her seat and sipped some coffee. 'Looks like, yes, but I wish I knew how he thought. How he feels. I'd give anything to know that.'

What she said disarmed me. It sounded honest and heartfelt. I tried to see her through Lily's super-cynical eyes. Couldn't quite manage it, but trying helped.

She took the photograph of William back and handled it almost reverently before pushing it towards me again. I got a whiff of something off-centre, almost erotic, as she looked down at the photo with her long, mascaraed lashes almost brushing her high cheekbones.

4

I wondered why Frank, who must have speculated about it when considering if he'd fathered another son, hadn't asked me to get a photo to check on the possibility of physical resemblance between himself and William Heysen.

With an abrupt gesture Catherine Heysen pushed the photos aside. 'Tell me this—do you look like your father?'

She had me there. I didn't, not in the least.

My expression told her what she wanted to hear. She made an expressive movement with her hands. There was something compelling, almost magnetic about her and it was easy to see how she'd coined it as a photographic model when younger. She could probably still make a go of it advertising certain products. I wasn't going to lose sight of the main question, but now that this matter had been opened up I thought I might as well pursue it.

'Your husband was a doctor. Wasn't he surprised when you got pregnant so quickly and had the child so soon?'

'William was late and large. He had to be induced. The time was . . . credible.'

'Heysen didn't know about Frank—that they'd . . . overlapped?'

She shook her head slightly; the shoulder-length, glossy dark hair shimmered and she smiled. 'My mother was Italian. I favour her as you can see. So does my oldest brother. The next brother favoured my father, who was Anglo. He was delighted and my husband—Gregory— spoke of hybrid vigour. William has blue eyes and his hair lightened as he grew older, although his skin is more olive than fair. Just a bit.'

Was there an edge of contempt in that? A sourness in her smile? I thought so. I was learning more about her all the time and the bits of knowledge seemed to contradict each other. Her self-control and confidence were almost complete but the mention of her son had opened a small chink in the armour. She was vain, with reason to be, but I had a feeling that her beauty hadn't made her happy. Ever.

'Why did you and Frank break up?'

'I'm sorry, but I don't think that's relevant or any of your business.'

'You're right. Okay. Let's get right down to it. Why are you so convinced your husband didn't arrange Bellamy's murder? The evidence that he did was pretty compelling.'

'The word of a dying man who'd been paid to bear false witness isn't compelling to my mind.'

'He was in financial difficulties and his partner's actions were undermining his practice. I've been told he was homophobic and had come to despise Bellamy.'

'That's true, but one thing, no, two things were totally neglected in the investigation. Gregory was what's now called a control freak, Mr Hardy. He was completely unable to delegate anything. That's why he worked such insane hours and why what Peter Bellamy was doing made him so angry. He'd worked twice as hard as Bellamy to build the practice, and now it was slipping downhill despite his efforts. If Gregory had intended to kill Bellamy he would have done it himself, not entrusted it to someone else. Talk to anyone who knew him and ask if he ever allowed another person to do something for him that he considered important.'

'That's interesting but it's hardly conclusive. Killing a person isn't an easy thing to do, Mrs Heysen. It's hard enough to do in war or in self-defence, let alone in cold blood. It's got its own psychology.'

She appeared to think that over briefly, then she said, 'I'm sure you speak from experience and know what you're talking about. But you're losing sight of Gregory's profession. I know for a fact that he killed a number of people. He was a believer in euthanasia.'

'Not the same.'

'Not quite, perhaps. But you spoke of the psychology of killing. Gregory didn't just send terminally ill people to sleep with morphine. He told me that he had killed several severely handicapped children and a man whom he regarded as dangerously insane.'

In a sense she was arguing against herself—if what she said was true then Heysen had the capacity to kill. But her point about him not delegating carried some weight. She saw that I was considering it and followed up.

'The other thing is this—think of how easy it would have been for Gregory to kill Peter himself if he'd wanted to. The drugs available to him . . .'

'They must have considered that in the investigation. What about at the trial?'

She gathered up the photographs, looking at them as if she'd never seen them before. She moved the photograph of her son closer to me across the table. 'His legal team was incompetent. The prosecution painted Gregory as a coward, unable to do his own dirty work. Of course, Gregory wasn't able to provide support for the idea that he could! This was twenty-three years ago, and you know how things stand with euthanasia even now.'

'Yes. How did they get the idea that he was a coward?'

Again, her smile had a bitter edge. 'Mr Hardy, my husband, as Frank must have told you, was a very dislike-able man.'

'In what way?'

'He was arrogant and conceited in all his dealings with people outside the practice. He treated people he regarded as his intellectual and social inferiors with contempt. And that was almost everyone. He rubbed everybody up the wrong way—the police, lawyers, the judge, the jurors—and it was his undoing.'

'He doesn't sound like a man you'd marry.'

She shrugged. 'Like Frank, he was manly. The fashion business is full of effeminates and pansies.'

Perhaps they were well suited, sharing at least one prejudice.

'I've got a couple more questions, if you're up to it.'

'I'm not a fragile person, Mr Hardy.'

'How did you manage to keep the boy unaware of what had happened to his father? I mean, you're still in the same house. There must have been talk.'

'After the appeal failed, I took William to Italy with me. That's where I did most of the modelling. It pays even better in Europe than here. I have family there on my mother's side. I took their name for professional reasons, Castilione. We stayed for nine years. We told William his father was dead. My family . . . connived, you might say, in this. When we came back the whole matter had died down. Neighbours here had moved away. You probably noticed all the apartment blocks. The whole area had changed. When Gregory died it hardly made a ripple, there was so much else going on. Memories are short.'

'That's true. The other question is, how did William find out the truth and how did he react?'

Frank had told me, but I wanted to hear it from her. Again, this was the sort of subject that shook her. Just a little. 'You must understand that William is . . . was a very energetic person. When we returned from Italy he set about adjusting to life here. He attended Cranbrook, where he was a first-class student and a fine sportsman. He was in the school teams for tennis and cricket and would have been for swimming if he'd been able to fit it in. He was popular and socially active as well.'

She drew a breath as if this catalogue of her son's qualities had tired her, but she went on almost at once. 'He did splendidly in the HSC in science subjects and languages. He could have got into medicine at Sydney, but he opted to study languages. He was fluent in Italian, of course, and true Italian, not a dialect. He studied French and Spanish and got a first-class degree. He went backpacking in Indonesia after finishing and he acquired a proficiency in Bahasa very easily.'

As someone who battled his way through school, especially at science and French, and dropped out of university, I was finding this Rhodes scholar stuff a bit hard to take. 'And did he live here through all this?' I asked.

'Oh, no. He lived in college and was only here in the holidays and sometimes at weekends and for family occasions. He was a favourite with the Italian side of my family, naturally. After university he moved into a flat with some other young people. He applied to the UN to work as a translator and was accepted as a trainee. While he was waiting for that to be arranged he worked at SBS, subtitling foreign films. He seemed so settled and stable with a career path ahead of him that I thought I should tell him the truth.'

'A version of it,' I said.

'Of course, you're right. I told him what had happened to his . . . my husband. I thought he was mature and confident enough to cope with it. I was wrong.'

Saying she was wrong was not something she liked doing. She paused, as if to try to think of some way to withdraw the admission, but there was none available. I was beginning to dislike her. I had no idea what she meant about true Italian and dialects, but it sounded snobbish. Again, it seemed as if she and Heysen had unpleasant characteristics in common. I started to question Frank's attraction to her, but maybe she was an actress and had projected a different personality to him.

'William went completely off the rails,' she said. 'He did some research and of course turned up the lurid tabloid stories about Gregory and all the details that came out at the trial. He turned against me for lying to him, and against the world he'd grown up in. He said he never wanted to see or hear from me again. He left his job and did not take up the traineeship at the UN. The last time I saw him he was heavily under the influence of drugs and he told me that selling them was how he made his living. That he was a criminal, just like his father. It broke my heart. I tried to tell him that Gregory wasn't guilty but he wouldn't listen.'

'Where is he now?'

'I have no idea.'

I had to think that over. The job seemed to be double-barrelled. What was the point of exonerating Gregory Heysen, in the unlikely event that that could be done, if the kid to give the good news to was missing?

'Have you tried to locate him?'

'How would I do that?'

'By hiring someone like me. Can't you see that this is two strands of the same story?'

'I hadn't thought of it that way . . . until now.'

'You have to consider every angle. What if William reconsidered? He's bright, you say. What if he's trying to find out more about Dr Heysen's conviction?'

'I suppose it's possible.'

'Which means he could be in danger.'

'Why?'

'You haven't thought this through, Mrs Heysen. If your husband was innocent, then someone framed him. Do you have any idea who that could be?'

I'd thought her story was thin in some way, and it was odd she hadn't tried to find the missing kid. Did she have some other agenda? But now she seemed genuinely alarmed.

'No.'

'Let's say you're right and your husband was framed or railroaded by whoever ordered the killing, or by the police, or both. If anyone starts poking around and finds things out, and the person or persons who arranged the frame-up learns of it . . .'

'I simply had not considered that.'

Her reaction didn't entirely convince me, but at least

she could imagine a scenario playing out in which she or her son or both could be at risk. She was silent for a few minutes and revealed her agitation by playing with the chains around her neck. I was tempted to go easy on her at this point but I held back, watching her and saying nothing.

'Are you going to help me . . . us?'

'I'll try, but you have to understand I'm more interested in helping Frank. You've thrown him into a spin.'

'I'm sorry,' she said, but I wasn't sure she was.

5

I told Catherine Heysen I'd keep her informed. She was
happy to see me go. As she ushered me out I wondered
how she spent her time. I didn't see any books where books
might have been. Getting herself tricked out must have
taken time but not all day. I had a sense that her life was as
empty as her house.

I had to hope my manner didn't cause her to bother
Frank, but I suspected they had an arrangement. I had a
number of people to see and this early in the piece there was
no particular priority: the order of approach was dictated
by geography and availability. Gregory Heysen's solicitor,
Michael Simmonds, had an office in Canterbury while Rex
Wain, one of the cops, since retired, who'd worked with
Frank, was in Marrickville. A toss-up.

I called Simmonds on my mobile. He was in court.
I got an appointment for mid-afternoon. Rex Wain I'd
run into a few times in the course of business. I had a
vague, unfavourable recollection of him as one of the
bully boys of whom there were so many back then. Frank
hadn't kept in touch but had asked around and got his
number. I got the voice message. I left my name and mobile

number and asked him to call. The other names on my list—the other ex-cops and cops still serving; the sister of Rafael Padrone, the man who'd fingered Heysen; the pathologist who'd testified about Bellamy's wounds; and several professional associates of the two doctors—were scattered about to all points of the compass.

In days gone by I would've killed the time until my appointment with the solicitor in a pub, but now I don't eat breakfast or lunch and keep my drinking till the evening—mostly, unless it's impolite to refuse. I decided to put in a little more work on Catherine Heysen herself and drove to Kingsgrove where Henry Hamil has his studio.

'Hercules' Henry, as he was known in his wrestling days, is a fashion photographer. I did some work for him a few years back, when a disgruntled model had hired a bunch of kids to steal Henry's equipment. The kids double-crossed the model and I got the equipment back cheaply. Henry and I had stayed in touch over the occasional drink and attendance at boxing nights.

Henry was as far from Catherine Heysen's stereotype of the effeminate photographer as it was possible to be. He was pushing sixty, twice married with two sets of kids, and kept himself fit by running. He'd had several successful exhibitions of his non-fashion photos, but he knew everybody in that world. No need to call him; he worked out of his studio and people came to him.

I climbed the steps to his studio, which had once been a cheese factory. Henry claimed he could sometimes still pick the smell of a ripe gorgonzola, but I'd never detected it. When I arrived he'd just finished a shoot and was disassembling the backdrop scenery with the help of Samantha, one of his daughters.

'Hey, Cliff,' he bellowed, 'come and lend a hand.'

I held and moved and stacked things for a few minutes until the job was done. Henry was massive in a white T-shirt and jeans. His hair was still thick and Aryan blond, but greying at the temples. Samantha was small and wiry, taking after her mother, but I wasn't sure which one.

'Off you go, love,' Henry said. 'The cheque's in the mail.'

'Dad.'

He took some notes from his wallet and handed them over. She kissed him on the cheek, waved to me and slid away.

'Probably spend it on unlistenable-to CDs,' Henry said. 'D'you like rap?'

I shuddered.

'Should listen to the words. It's worse than you think. What's up, Cliff? Coffee?'

'I've just had a couple of cups of the best coffee I've ever tasted, Henry. Wouldn't want to lose the buzz. You go ahead.'

'Fuck it, I've been working since six am. What about a cold one?'

We settled in a couple of canvas-backed director's chairs with a can each. Henry reached for the ceiling and rotated his trunk slowly, easing his close to muscle-bound frame. He took a long pull on his can.

'Are you going to invite me to Anthony Mundine's next outing to which you have free tickets, you and many others?'

'No.'

'What a disappointment. So?'

'I'm wondering if you know anything about a model

working here in the early nineties. Very beautiful. Italian-looking. Catherine Heysen, or maybe Beddoes.'

'Doesn't ring a bell.'

'Hang on, she told me she worked under another name in Europe. Castilone, something like that.'

Henry snapped his fingers. 'Now you're talking—CC we called her, Catherine Castilione. Now that was one beautiful woman. Wonderful bones. Are you working for her?'

'Not exactly. Did you photograph her?'

'Only a couple of times. I heard she came into some money and retired.'

'Would you still have the shot or shots?'

'Of course. I've got nearly everything I've done on disc. Young Sam, who you just saw helping, did it for me. Want to see?'

We went over to his computer and he began clicking keys. The images were minutely catalogued and within a few minutes he had those in question up on the screen. One set showed a tall, slender woman in a simple black dress with a string of pearls around her neck. The advertisement was for the pearls but it was hard to take your eyes off the woman's face and body. She looked like the young Sophia Loren and, while there was nothing provocative about her pose, she exuded sex appeal. In another series, she was modelling a severely cut trouser suit. Same effect.

'Not bad, eh? See the bone structure? Lighting a face like that's a sheer pleasure. How's she look now?'

'Just as good, in an older way.'

'Doesn't surprise me. She'll look good till the day she dies, and after that.'

'D'you remember much about her? I mean, what she said about herself, what you talked about on the shoot?'

Henry shook his head. 'I could hardly get a word out of her. All I remember is that she was an unhappy person. Doesn't really matter in this game. Don't want them to look too happy.'

'She was making a lot of money, she said.'

'Not that much. The trouble with her was that she looked so good the suspicion was the customers wanted her rather than the product. Different in Europe, where she wouldn't have looked so exotic.'

'Did she ever mention her son?'

'Now that's something I'd forgotten. She brought him along to the suit session. Nice enough looking kid, very much like her, not a lot of his dad in him, I guess. Well behaved. As I recall, he sat and read a book.'

'A twelve-year-old boy reading a book? What kind of book? What about?'

Henry shrugged. 'Can't remember, probably didn't ask. A proper book. Hard cover.'

'What was their relationship like?'

Henry drained his can. 'Hard to say. They didn't talk much, and then it was in Italian. I no speak. Respectful?'

'That all?'

'What're you getting at?'

'I'm not sure.'

Still with time to kill, I drove back to the Heysen house in Earlwood. I stopped a short distance from it and tried to look at it again through fresh eyes. I still wasn't convinced that a woman like her would choose to stay in such a white elephant of a house. Some of the things she'd told me had checked out solidly with Henry Hamil, but I was by no means sure that she'd told me the truth about everything. Was there some complication regarding the title to the house? Did that explain her hanging on to it over the years? Did she stay there now in the hope her son would contact her there and she'd lose that chance if she moved away? I made a note of it as just one of a number of things I'd have to check with Frank while deceiving Hilde. It wasn't going to be much fun.

Michael Simmonds, the solicitor, was a small man in his sixties who looked as if time was pecking away at him piece by piece—hair, body, voice. But his mind was sharp and his memory for events twenty-plus years ago was acute.

'Horatio Mallory,' he said in his reedy tones in answer to my question about Gregory Heysen's barrister, 'was arrogant, superior and bombastic. He met his match in Heysen, and together they destroyed any semblance of a defence that could have been mounted.'

We were in his office in Canterbury Road, a suite three floors up in a new building with all mod cons. Simmonds, dressed in a suit with a waistcoat, explained that his partner and paralegals did most of the work these days and that he was semi-retired.

'But I keep my hand in, Mr Hardy. Had a goodish win this morning. I miss the cut and thrust. Don't miss the conveyancing, I must say. I've had a bit to do in my time with chaps in your profession. Some stories I could tell you, but I suppose you've heard them all.'

I guess it was nostalgia for the old, heady days that had led him to make me so welcome, or perhaps it was the good win. We were settled in comfortable chairs in a small

meeting room adjacent to his office and the cup of coffee
I had, although inferior to Catherine Heysen's, was acceptable on a day that had turned cold and blustery. I ran a few
names past Simmonds. He didn't remember Frank Parker
but Rex Wain rang a bell.

'I didn't take to him,' Simmonds said. 'Pushy, with bad
grammar. You have, if I may say so, an altogether more
soothing manner despite your rough exterior.'

'And here's me thinking I was looking my best to call on
the Widow Heysen.'

He smiled. 'Forgive me. I'm old-fashioned, as you see.
I take off my tie to go to bed.'

He said he was surprised that Catherine Heysen was still
pursuing the matter. His pale, watery eyes behind the thick
lenses retained a keenness about them. He was one of those
men—and I'd met a few—that you didn't lie to because you
knew they'd trip you up. Without giving him chapter and
verse, I indicated that I was working for another involved
party and that had captured his interest and led him to
open up so frankly about the late Horatio Mallory.

'What might that defence have been?'

'It would have been difficult at the best of times, with
that chap's confession. What was his name again?'

'Rafael Padrone.'

'Just so. His statement was plausible, perfectly recorded
and documented, and Mallory floundered trying to
counteract it. I advised a cautious approach, to try and tease
out the possibility that someone else might have put
Padrone up to it, that perhaps he was under some kind of
pressure. But poor old Horatio went at it bull-at-a-gate—
blackening Padrone's name, disparaging his background,
his ethnicity. There were a couple of people of Italian

descent on the jury. A shambles. And it wasn't a propitious time for defending doctors.'

I tried to cast my mind back but couldn't recall any particularly anti-medico sentiment at the time, other than cartoons suggesting that they didn't make house calls because they were too busy playing golf.

Simmonds smiled. 'Can't remember, eh? I can. It's far enough back. I'm in that condition where past events are crystal clear and I can't recall what I had for lunch. Not quite, but you know what I mean.'

'We all get there.'

'Just so. Well, as I say, it wasn't a good time to be appearing for a doctor accused of a serious crime. It never is, really. The public rates the profession very highly but takes a dim view when a member of it transgresses. Anyway, there'd recently been a scandal involving doctors in car crash insurance fraud and the Medicare system had recently been modified with the result that some doctors—surgeons, I think—had gone on strike.'

I nodded. 'It's coming back to me. I seem to remember that doctors had a few problems back around then. There was Edelsten and his pink helicopter lifestyle, and Nick Paltos, who got sucked in by the gamblers and tried drug importation as a way out. That sleep therapy nutter couldn't have helped the image.'

'Not a bit, and when Heysen presented, all puffed up with his own importance, you can imagine the reaction. I suppose you're wondering why a suburban solicitor was brought in on such a serious matter?'

'I have a feeling you'd have been up to it.'

'I was in those days. I did a bit of criminal work, some of it fairly high profile. But the fact is that we handled the conveyancing when Heysen bought the Earlwood house. Not a difficult job, because, for a youngish doctor not long in practice, he had substantial equity. Of course, that was before they had to pay back the cost of their degrees. One of my then partners steered it through and Heysen seemed to have confidence in us, so he came to me when the police homed in on him. Mallory was a mistake. He would not have been my choice, but Heysen had met him somewhere and insisted on him.'

'Did Heysen's wife attend the trial? I forgot to ask her.'

'Indeed she did, and added to the ill-feeling. She was dressed to the nines, glamour personified, and induced resentment among the female jurors and lust among the males. Altogether unfortunate.'

'It sounds like a nightmare from where you were sitting.'

'Yes, especially as old Horatio was so taken with the wife that he could hardly keep his mind on the business. The joke around the place at the time—trials are full of jokes, as you'd know from experience and television—was that Mallory wanted his client to lose so that he might get a free run at the wife. Nonsense, of course.'

I liked this man. 'You're being very frank, Mr Simmonds.'

'Indiscreet, you mean.'

I shrugged. 'I'm grateful.'

'No mystery. I've heard of you, Mr Hardy. I remember that Viv Garner represented you at the hearing you had to attend in connection with your licence.'

I nodded. A recent case where the police had found me less than cooperative and insisted that I go before the licensing board. 'A suspension,' I said. 'I took a holiday.'

'So Viv told me. We're old acquaintances. I've got a lot of time for him. Odd expression, in the context of our profession.'

'I've done some—once on remand and a short stretch.'

'Inevitable, I'd say, for an energetic enquiry agent, especially back when the police were more corrupt than at present. The point is, Viv Garner vouched for you in the highest terms, so I felt I should be as helpful as possible. However, I'm not sure that I have been.'

Viv Garner had been my solicitor for some years and had seen me through some scrapes in which you could have said I was culpable, and some that were merely misinterpretations. 'You have been,' I said. 'My understanding is that Padrone had pleaded guilty.'

'That's so.'

'But he could have paid for a defence.'

'What's your point?'

'Just that he must have made some sort of deal on his sentence and treatment.'

'I suppose so, but I know nothing about it.'

'After what you've told me I think I can probably put one more question to you.'

We'd finished the coffee, but Simmonds was a man with a taste for the dramatic. He lifted what must have been an empty cup to his mouth before he spoke: 'I can anticipate it—do I think Dr Gregory Heysen was guilty of the charge of conspiracy to commit murder?'

'Right.'

'I do not.'

'Why?'

'The man was highly intelligent. I mean exceptionally so. His academic record showed that and I spoke to one of

his professors who said that Heysen could have made a bril-
liant medical researcher, capable perhaps of major work.'

'All news to me.'

'None of this came out at the trial. Heysen refused to
allow the professor to give evidence. Can you guess why?'

'Tell me.'

'At this point I was almost sorry for Mallory. Heysen
said the man was a Jew and second-rate as a scientist and
teacher.'

'Jesus.'

'If Gregory Heysen had arranged the death of Peter
Bellamy, I'm quite sure no one would ever have suspected
him of it. He would have contrived it in a far more clever
way.'

'A hard defence to put up, that.'

'Oh, Heysen would have been all for it, but in that
event his sentence was more likely to have been twenty
years rather than fourteen.'

'All things considered, fourteen years seems a bit light.'

Simmonds shook his head. 'Prejudice against homosexuals and the beginnings of the AIDS hysteria. For all
Judge Montague-Brown detested Heysen, he probably hated
homosexuals more.'

I shook my head. 'Lawyers. Sorry.'

'Don't be. We're just a necessary evil. But you've jogged
my memory. I recall thinking that the police were very . . .
ardent. Almost as if they—'

'Had planted evidence? I've seen that.'

'No. Let me think. Don't put words in my mouth. As if
they had something else on Heysen and were determined to
get him, one way or another.'

6

Rex Wain didn't call. I went to the Redgum gym in Leichhardt for a workout and then to the Bar Napoli for a coffee. Over the long black, I called two of the other cops who'd been on the Heysen case. The Telstra voice told me that one of the numbers was no longer operating and when I called the other I got a takeaway Chinese food outlet in Carlton. Frank's information was sadly out of date.

The day had turned from blustery to stormy with big black clouds piling up against each other. I drove home to batten down the hatches. A big branch from a camphor laurel tree had been brushing against one of the windows and I'd resolved to lop it before the next high wind in case it did serious damage. Of course, I'd put that action off for weeks, months.

I got home before the sky opened, changed into jeans, a T-shirt and sneakers, and put an aluminium ladder up against the wall of the house. I applied an old, rusted bush saw to the branch. Working upwards is not the way to go but my ladder only reached so far. My father had tried to instruct me as a handyman, but I'd found passing him nails and changing between the Phillips head and the other kind of screwdriver so boring I closed off. Occasionally I regretted not having the facility.

'A workman is only as good as his tools,' he used to say. He was right. I never had the right tools for that kind of work.

With the sky darkening and the light dropping, I sawed away in the confined space at the side of the house. I was being scratched by thorny branches and sweat was running into my eyes.

I'm going to flog this place, I thought. Get a unit at Coogee and let the body corporate handle the maintenance.

'Hey, Hardy.'

I was standing on top of the ladder none too securely and, surprised by the voice, I almost fell. As it was I dropped the saw. Bracing myself against the wall, I looked down. Rex Wain was standing three metres below me with his hand on the ladder.

'Gidday, Wain,' I said. 'You bloody nearly made me fall.'

He gave the ladder a gentle shake. 'That's exactly what I'm fucking going to do. Let's see you piss me around with a broken leg.'

'What're you talking about?'

'You fucking know.'

He bent to pick up the saw and took his hand off the ladder. I went down two rungs quickly and jumped. He swore and swung at me with the saw but he was slow and impeded by the branches of the shrubs. I ducked under the wing and bullocked into him, forcing him back against the wall. He dropped the saw. I hit him hard about where his right kidney was and he gasped. I jerked his left arm up his back and held him there, pressing his head against the bricks.

'You're out of shape, Rex. Had enough?'

'Fuck you.'

'Only reason I phoned you was to talk about an old case. That's it. Nothing else. Now you can believe me and come in have a drink or you can have another go and get knocked about. Up to you.'

He muttered something I couldn't catch.

'What was that?'

A couple of fat raindrops fell as a prelude to some heavy stuff coming.

He eased his mouth away from the wall and turned his head towards me. 'Nothing about the Logan business?' His breath stank of booze and bad teeth.

'No.'

'Okay, then. Sorry, sorry.'

I let him go and picked up the saw. 'Let's go inside before it pisses down. No tricks, Rex. A scratch from this rusty blade and you're a tetanus case, for sure.'

'No worries.'

I shepherded him around to the front of the house and we went in and down the passage to the kitchen at the back on the ground floor. Wain was a good ten years older than me and not wearing well. His sandy hair was thin on top and his belly ballooned his shirt front out over his belt. He wore a light grey suit that could have done with a clean and was missing buttons. He rubbed the spot where I'd hit him and stroked his nose. His face had hit the wall pretty hard.

I sat him down at the kitchen bench and gave him a solid scotch. He shook his head when I offered him ice, and tossed it down in one gulp. I poured another and one for myself. The rain came, thundering on the iron roof of the bathroom behind the kitchen—an add-on long after the house was built.

'Who's Logan?' I said.

'Shit, it doesn't matter. Just a pissed-off client. I got into your game after I left the force. I thought he might have hired you to get his money back or something.'

'You don't seem to be doing too well at it.'

He tasted his drink this time and looked around the room. 'You're not exactly coining it yourself. This isn't a single malt and this joint's a dump. Worth a bit though, I suppose.'

'How about we have the talk I wanted to have, since you're here?'

Wain was regaining his confidence. He picked bits of shrub and leaf from his jacket and deposited them on the bench. 'What's in it for me?'

'Are things that bad, that a professional discussion attracts a fee?'

'Matter of principle, Hardy, you prick. Never liked you and still don't.'

'It's mutual, Rex. Let's say I ask you some questions, and depending on your answers I decide whether what you say is worth any of my client's money. Otherwise, finish your drink and get on your bloody bike.'

The recovered confidence was tissue-thin. He drained his glass and pushed it at me. 'Okay. I'll have a bit of ice and water this time.'

It took over an hour and half a bottle of scotch to get anything useful out of him. He hadn't been the senior man on the Heysen murder but he'd done a lot of legwork and had sat in on all the briefings and progress reports. He was convinced that Heysen was guilty of hiring Padrone to do the wet work.

'Why?' I said.

'We talked to the sister, this hooker. Pammy, Priscilla . . . Pixie, that's it. William Street prostie. She reckoned Padrone told her he'd done it and that he was going to give her some of the money. Said she never got it, but we thought she was lying.'

I cast my mind back to the trial reports. 'That didn't come out at the trial.'

Wain shook his head. 'Cassidy, the D heading us up— he's dead by the way—was real pissed off about that. She shot through. We couldn't find her. Couldn't make anything of it, like. But it firmed us up on Heysen, you know how it is.'

I did, and I wondered if this lay behind Simmonds' idea that the police had more on Heysen than they could use.

'Go on.'

'With what?'

'You put the case together—means, motive, opportunity. What was Padrone's motive?'

'Shit, no worries there. He was dying of cancer and Heysen had been the only one to offer him anything. He offered to pay him enough so he could go to Germany for this special treatment. Padrone hated doctors anyway. Got the dough, did the job and then couldn't get permission to travel. He was fucked and he knew it, so he decided to take Heysen with him. End of story.'

Wain poured more whisky and water. When he drank it he showed the brownish teeth of a heavy smoker. He wasn't smoking now and his fingers weren't stained. He didn't seem like the type to have given up voluntarily, and I concluded he simply couldn't afford it. Wouldn't improve his mood.

'You haven't told me much.'

'Why the fuck should I? All you've given me is a shove around and some third-rate scotch. I don't even know why you're interested in this old shit.'

'You don't need to know. I was thinking of giving you some money if you could . . .'

'Do what? I'm on the bones of my arse, Hardy.'

'Your phone rings.'

'Christ knows why. I haven't paid the bill in months. Can't be long before I get cut off. Come on, what d'you want? I'll give it to you if I can.'

He reached for the bottle but I moved it away. It was just a feeling but the way he'd said end of story didn't play with me—didn't sound right for him.

'There was something more about Heysen, wasn't there? I know he was a prick who no one liked, that he treated you all like shit. I hear what you say about the sister's evidence that you couldn't produce. But I've got a feeling there was something more. Something to hide.'

That almost seemed to sober him. He rubbed at his bloodshot, defeated eyes and his shoulders slumped. He behaved as if he was looking down a long tunnel with no turning and no light at the end of it. 'Jesus Christ,' he mumbled. 'I thought just me and Cassidy . . .'

I poured myself a drink. 'Yes?'

'It's time to talk money.'

'I could go a couple of hundred.'

He shook his head and regretted doing it. 'Way too low.'

I considered. He wasn't an actor. 'Three.'

'Six.'

'Five tops.'

'Okay. Let's see it.'

'We'll have to go to an ATM. Time you were on your way anyhow.'

'Let's go. You can drop me at the ATM.'

'How'd you get here?'

'Fucking bus.'

'We'll walk. I've had a bit too much on an empty stomach to drive.'

He sneered at me, the confidence returning again.

The heavy rain had stopped. I put on a jacket and we walked to the Commonwealth Bank ATM in Glebe Point Road. Wain shambled along. He'd never been a solid performer as a detective, either police or private, but now he was a ruin. I drew out the money and we stood on the steps of the bank with the evening traffic passing and the people out to eat Thai, Italian, Indian, Lebanese, whatever, strolling by. The rain started again, lighter.

I held the folded notes in my hand. 'What was the whisper, Rex?'

There was no one close, but he looked around furtively. He appeared to be about to speak but he kept quiet. He cleared his throat and the sound was like a groan crossed with a whimper. I could smell his foul breath and the rain brought out the mustiness of his clothes. He looked hungrily at the money, then shook his head.

'Can't do it,' he muttered.

'We had a deal.'

'Fuck the deal. I can't do it.'

'I might go up a bit if the information's good.'

He laughed. 'There isn't enough money in this fucking bank.'

He meant it. He took a step away and turned up his collar. I handed him a fifty. He took it and stumbled down the steps into the drizzle.

7

I phoned the Parkers and got Hilde.

'Hello, Cliff. Haven't seen you for a bit. Been busy?'

'Yeah. How are you, love?'

'I've got my bloody time of life which isn't much fun.'

'Bit young for that, aren't you?'

'You're losing track of time. I'll be okay. I'm trying some herbal stuff that's said to be good. When're we going to see you?'

'Soon, I hope. Is Frank around? I need a bit of help with something.'

'I'll get him. Make it soon.'

No outright lies there, but close.

'Hello, Cliff. Results already?'

'Hardly,' I said. I decided to work my way towards the subject—an old habit. 'A couple of things I'm interested in. Padrone's medical records. Nothing about them in your notes.'

'I should've mentioned that—they went missing. Heysen was happy to produce them but they couldn't be found.'

I skimmed through the pages of Frank's notes. 'What

about this receptionist—Roma Brown? Didn't she know what happened to them?'

'Cassidy interviewed her, not me. He was a sloppy cop. Fat slob. God knows how he got the rank he did.'

'Corrupt?'

'Back then, who knows? Anyway, he said she didn't have a clue. You think the records are important?'

'Dunno. How about Rex Wain?'

'What about him?'

'Was he any good?'

'Better than Cassidy.'

'Not as good as you?'

'Modesty forbids. He was all right. Thick as . . . I was going to say thick as thieves with Damien Cassidy, but I never heard they were on the take. Why the interest?'

I told him about my interview with Wain, how down on his luck he was and how he and Cassidy seemed to know something about the Heysen case that no one else did. Something he wouldn't tell me for any money. Frank was quiet, taking this in.

'Frank?'

'It wouldn't be the first time senior police kept secrets from juniors. Not always dodgy either. There can be valid reasons. But this sounds strange. You believed him?'

'He wanted the money like a dog wants a bone. He *needed* it.'

Frank said he hadn't a clue what the hidden information might be. He hadn't been full-time on the Heysen case but he'd attended most of the briefings and thought he was in the picture. I said it was an angle I'd have to do some work on. He sounded depressed when he responded—understandably, thinking back to the state of the police force in those days—so I didn't tell him his information on the other detectives was out of date.

'How's Hilde?' I said.

'Okay. I'll put her back on. She wants to talk to you.'

That was a worry—had she twigged that something was being hidden from her?

'Cliff, I just wanted to know if you were still with Lily,' she said.

'Ah, the word *with* doesn't quite cut it. She's still staying here while her place gets fixed up. She's away at the moment, in Adelaide. But . . . it's going well.'

'Good. Bring her over for a meal.'

I said I would and rang off.

It was interesting that Padrone's medical records were missing. Interesting, but what it pointed to I had no idea. I rang Catherine Heysen.

'Mrs Heysen, Cliff Hardy. I'm wondering if you remember a woman named Roma Brown.'

'No.'

A minion, not worth remembering.

'She was the receptionist at your husband's surgery.'

'Oh, yes. I remember now.'

'Do you happen to know where she lived? I want to talk to her. Perhaps your husband had a Teledex or something?'

'He did. The police took it and never returned it. But I remember that she lived very close by. The surgery was in Crown Street, and I recall Gregory saying she was never late because she lived just around the corner. He was a stickler for being prompt. But what street he meant I don't know.'

'Thank you. That's a help.'

'Have you made any . . . progress?'

'I hope so. Goodnight.'

I brought my notes and expenses up to date. Fifty bucks for Rex Wain. No receipt.

That night the storm picked up again and the branch I'd sawn at came crashing down. The noise woke me and I checked on the window. Intact. I made a mental note to retrieve the ladder and do something about the branch, but my mental notes don't always get acted on.

Next day I located an address for Roma Brown in a mid-1980s electoral roll in the Mitchell Library. The address checked with one of the many R. Browns in the phone book. She was in Burton Street, which meets Crown just below Oxford, so it all fitted. I rang the number without expecting to get her in business hours but she answered. I explained my call by saying that I was working with a police officer writing a book about some of his old cases, such as the murder of Dr Bellamy, and wanted to tie up some loose ends. She gave a little yelp of pleasure.

'I'd be delighted to see you, Mr Hardy. I haven't got many distractions these days, apart from my little hobby. When do you want to come?'

I was only a hop-skip-and-a-jump away, so we agreed on half an hour to give me time to find a park. The block of flats dated back a bit, to the sixties maybe, with the plain lines and absence of extra comforts of that time. No balconies. I buzzed her flat and she released the heavy security door. I ignored the lift and went up the four flights of stairs for the cardiovascular benefit. At her door I buzzed again and she opened it with the chain on.

'Mr Hardy?'

I looked down. She was in a wheelchair. I showed her my PEA licence and she undid the chain.

'Do come in.' She backed the wheelchair expertly and we went down a short passage to a small living room with a minimum of furniture to allow her to get about. She pointed to a chair and drew her wheelchair up in front of me so that our knees weren't far from touching. She was in her fifties, good-looking in a fair, faded kind of way, and very thin. She wore a neat grey dress and black shoes that looked expensive. In fact nothing in the room looked cheap.

'Have you ever been in a wheelchair, Mr Hardy?'

'Once or twice.'

'I've been in one for twenty years. I had a car accident.'

'I'm sorry.'

'Yes, so am I, but I was lucky. The man who hit me was very wealthy and heavily insured so I wasn't left destitute. That gets all that embarrassing disability stuff out of the way.'

'I'm not embarrassed,' I said. 'In your place I'd probably be a cringing alcoholic mess. You're not and I admire you.'

'That's kind, but you might surprise yourself. Pray God it never happens. Now what did you want to know about Dr Heysen and poor Dr Bellamy? I *am* intrigued.'

An interesting choice of words, I thought, and it clearly indicated whose side she was on. But the lie about a book being written had struck the right note. Bookcases in the sitting room were filled to bursting. I squinted at the titles.

'I'm interested in the missing medical records for Rafael Padrone. Do you remember anything about that?'

She paused, and for a minute I thought she was going to close up, but she was only collecting her thoughts. Some of them must have been pleasant because she smiled and something of the prettiness she must have had in her youth came back into her face. 'I remember quite a lot. I particularly remember the police officer who interviewed me. Do you know that he sat in my office and smoked without asking my permission and that he picked his teeth.'

'Cassidy,' I said. 'You can say whatever you want about him because he's dead. I'm told he wasn't mannerly.'

'That's putting it mildly, but I have nothing more to say about him. Well, he asked for the Padrone file and I looked for it and couldn't find it and he became very rude. He virtually accused me of stealing it. "Why would I do that?" I said, but he wasn't the sort of person to reason with.'

'Do you know who took the records?'

'I have a very good idea. Another policeman came who was more polite, but I still didn't tell him my suspicion.'

'Why not?'

The rejuvenating smile again. 'I wasn't a middle-aged cripple back then, Mr Hardy. I was a lively woman. I was a very good dancer.'

'I believe you,' I said. 'Also intelligent.' I pointed to the bookcases. 'I can see George Eliot, Trollope, Lawrence, Waugh, Martin Boyd . . .'

'Have you read them?'

'Bits of, not as much as you. I was more Conrad, Stevenson, Maugham, Hemingway, Idriess.'

She nodded. 'Some strange things went on in that surgery. I was concerned, but it was a very good job, well paid, convenient to where I lived, and I liked Dr Bellamy very much. I wasn't medically trained, I couldn't judge the . . . ethics.'

'Yes?'

'I'm guessing, from glimpses of some of the people I saw arriving after hours, but I know Dr Heysen had developed techniques for removing tattoos and scars. I suspect he also . . . altered people's appearance.'

That wasn't what I was expecting but was still interesting, maybe even more so. I couldn't understand why this outwardly respectable woman wouldn't have said something about it to the police, once the shit had hit the fan.

She put on the spectacles she wore on a chain around her neck, stared directly at me, and I had to struggle to look her in the eye. 'I was in love,' she said.

'With Heysen?'

'That conceited cold fish? No.'

'Bellamy?'

She laughed. 'Very attractive, but a lost cause. No, with Dr Karl Lubeck.'

'I haven't heard of him.'

'Well, he was sort of an assistant to Dr Heysen and I suppose you'd say he was employed on a casual basis. Things were much looser then, before the GST and all that.'

'You think he took the records?'

'He might have. There were other files missing. I didn't tell the police about them either. I . . . I assume they were for these . . . after-hours people Dr Heysen and Karl—Dr Lubeck—dealt with and that Mr Padrone's file was taken too, perhaps by mistake.'

She sat quietly while I absorbed this. We were both lost in thought, though of very different kinds. She'd given me a whole new perspective on Heysen, one that hadn't come out from Catherine Heysen or in the police investigation, but very possibly what Rex Wain had been afraid to talk about.

She broke the silence. 'I didn't think it mattered. Padrone killed Dr Bellamy and confessed to doing it on Dr Heysen's behalf. I believed that.'

'Do you still believe it, Ms Brown?'

'Yes, why not? But at the time I was more concerned about my broken heart. I didn't say anything about Karl in order to protect him. Love is blind.'

'It is,' I said. 'Part of the fun. So you went on seeing him?'

'For a very short while. Then he told me he had to go overseas to deal with something. He sent postcards. Then nothing. I was hurt and I had no job. Not much money and I had to get on with my life. And I did. I put Karl and his sweet talk behind me. I had other lovers. Then my accident happened a few years later. After that it was hospitals and operations and recovery, ups and downs and . . .'

'I understand.'

'I was renting this flat. I was able to buy it with the insurance money. The prices weren't so outrageous then. I had the little idea that Karl might come back to look for me. This was where we'd met and made love. But he never did.'

'I'm going to have to ask you about him. Will that upset you?'

She let loose a throaty laugh. 'Not in the least. I don't want you to think I'm a dried-up, frustrated old woman, Mr Hardy.'

Her eyes were bright and her smile had turned mocking—at me.

'I don't,' I said.

'You might. You couldn't be blamed.' She consulted a gold watch on her wrist. 'Yes. This's a good time. Let me show you something.'

She wheeled around and moved towards a door standing ajar. Her bedroom. The room had a big window with a view across the street to a block of flats of similar size and vintage.

'Sit on the bed,' she said. 'A great big fellow like you would be too obvious.'

Directly opposite and not more than fifty metres away was another large window. I had a clear view into the room and saw a tall, blonde woman taking off her dress and unhooking her bra to reveal impressive breasts. A man standing near her was watching with his hands busy on himself.

'Not a good one,' Roma Brown said. 'A disappointment. Probably just a self-abuser. It's better when they do something standing up or they have oral sex. That's very enjoyable. Are you shocked?'

If I was, I wasn't going to show it. 'I'm surprised she doesn't know about you.'

The wheelchair spun around again and she laughed as she left the room. 'Oh, she knows. We're quite good friends. She doesn't mind in the least. In fact she says it gives her pleasure. As you can imagine, not every engagement is enjoyable. It's what I meant by my little hobby.'

We went back to the sitting room. 'I just wanted you to know that although Karl broke my heart and a motor car broke my body, I haven't resigned from the human race. A very nice man visits me regularly and we enjoy ourselves— well, I certainly do.'

'I'm glad to hear it. Tell me about Dr Lubeck—Karl. German, I suppose.'

'Originally, I'm sure. But he had no accent. He was as Australian as you and I with our standard names. I must admit I knew very little about him. The affair only lasted a few weeks.'

'You don't have a photograph?'

'I did, but I tore it up in pique. I'm sorry. He was tall, like you, and dark like you. But more heavily built and with much less hair. Very little, in fact. I've never found baldness unattractive, which men don't understand.'

'They say bald men have more testosterone.'

She smiled. 'Well, he certainly had his share. What else? I got the impression he was a contemporary of Dr Heysen and Dr Bellamy and had qualified at Sydney University. I mean contemporary as a graduate—Karl was a few years older.'

'Family?'

'Never mentioned. D'you mean did he have a wife? After what happened, I wouldn't be surprised. Shouldn't you be making notes?'

'Later. Habits? Sports? Interests?'

'Mr Hardy, I was head over heels in blind love. I'd be inventing if I said that from my point of view the answer to your questions was anything but sex, sex, sex.'

8

I went to the outdoor coffee area where Burton Street hits Crown, ordered a flat white and sat down with my notebook to make my usual squiggles, arrows and dotted lines. They're supposed to help me make connections and to inspire questions and speculations. Sometimes they do, and once or twice the process has led me definitively through a maze in the right direction. Mostly, they just help to make the maze clearer.

Roma Brown was a fresh source, virtually untapped by the police. If Wain or one of the other PEAs had talked to her she certainly would have mentioned it. A fresh source when investigating an old matter on which the dust has settled is pure gold. She'd given me things to think about. If she was right about Heysen doing makeovers of some sort for shady customers, it could explain why he had the substantial equity Simmonds had mentioned. Equally, it could have put him in danger if one of his clients was either dissatisfied or took it into his head to take the doctor out of circulation. The possibilities were many.

A complication to this line of thinking was the evidence that Heysen was strapped for cash at the time of Bellamy's death. Had the makeover business dried up? And if so, why? Was he being blackmailed? And if so, by whom?

All that was assuming that someone had framed Heysen for Bellamy's murder. But what if Bellamy had found out about his partner's illicit activities and had hired Padrone to silence him and been outbid by Heysen? Guilty as charged, but a tangled and very speculative web. If Cassidy and Wain had known about Heysen's sideline and hushed it up, what might've followed from that? Getting to be too much to hold in my head. I drank the coffee and sketched out the various scenarios as a series of questions. One course of action was clear—find Karl Lubeck, the medical Lothario.

The coffee tables and umbrellas were located in a space dropped down below the level of Crown Street that's reached by a set of sandstone steps. A bit of old Sydney town preserved—something I always like to see. A much-touted vegetarian restaurant is opposite, along with boutiques and minute art galleries. There are plenty of sex shops around selling what they sell, and I suppose people seeing Roma Brown in her wheelchair would think they were irrelevant to her. They'd be dead wrong, I thought, and good on her.

Back in the Mitchell Library, and I set about the task of tracking Dr Karl methodically, consulting first the telephone directories in all the capital cities, knowing the reluctance of doctors to go bush. No result. Then the medical directory which covers the whole country and is never completely up to date but catches most of the long-termers. Ditto.

I stood on the steps outside the library as the rain fell,

and rang my doctor, Ian Sangster, who sits on various medical boards and tribunals and has extensive contacts in the profession.

'This was when?' Ian asked.

'Twenty-three years ago.'

'Could be dead, it's a high stress profession.'

'He'd only be sixty or so.'

'What was his lifestyle?'

'All I know is that he liked sex and I'm told he was good at it.'

'That's a life-preserving recipe. Sorry, Cliff, never heard of him, but I'll ask around. D'you know anything more about him? Any chance he was deregistered somewhere along the line?'

'Possible, but that's all I've got at present.'

'I can check that. I'll let you know if he turns up.'

Not much more to be done there for the moment. There was no mention of a Dr Lubeck in Frank's notes or at the trial. Either the police didn't find out about him or Cassidy and Wain knew of him but suppressed the information. Why? Maybe because they were concealing everything to do with Heysen's sideline. Again, why? Good question. Possible answers were a pay-off or fear. On the basis of Wain's reaction, I'd have to go along with fear. But of whom or what?

Another name I had a question mark beside was Pixie Padrone. I was still curious about what had happened to the alleged fee for the hit. I added a question mark beside the twenty grand. Wain had said that Pixie was on the street, meaning that she was in the lower echelon of sex workers—the least paid, the most exploited, the most vulnerable. In that shadowy world people disappear, change their names, change their sex and are hard to track.

I had a source of information though—Ruby Gentle is the proprietor of the House of Ruby, a massage parlour and relaxation centre in Kings Cross. I'd located her lost daughter some years back, got a protection racketeer off her back, and we've remained on friendly terms. I hadn't seen her since I'd left Darlinghurst for Newtown, but this was definitely the time to renew the acquaintance.

The House of Ruby is open twenty-four hours a day and Ruby herself is in attendance until the early hours in a supervisory and occasionally participatory capacity. It was mid-afternoon on a Friday and I knew she'd be there.

I hit the buzzer beside the gate in Darlinghurst Road and the voice spoke softly just above my right ear.

'Can I help you?'

'You can tell Ruby that Cliff Hardy is here to see her, thank you.'

After a few minutes the gate swung open and I went through the scrap of garden to the front door, which clicked open as I approached. The woman behind the desk was typical of Ruby's receptionists—thirty plus, smartly turned out, expertly made up and with a pleasant voice and manner. 'She said to go upstairs, Mr Hardy, and that you know your way.'

'I do, thanks.'

Your two-storey Victorian terraces all follow much the same pattern on the upper level, with a large room in front, usually with a balcony, and other smaller rooms off a corridor going towards the back. The design is ideal for a brothel and a good many of them have served that purpose. Ruby, naturally, occupied the front room where she'd installed an ensuite and partitioned off a cubbyhole for her office. The remaining space isn't subtle in decor—a big four-poster bed with silk and satin trappings, two padded, velvet covered chairs, a wall mirror, a cabinet for professional equipment and a television with VCR and DVD players.

The door was standing open and I walked in. Ruby rose from a chair and sailed towards me like a galleon in a strong wind. She stands close to 180 centimetres in her stilettos and weighs close to 100 kilos. Wrapped in flowing draperies—'Rubensesque' is how she describes herself—that description about does it. She has black hair, pale skin and heavy, handsome features all owing a great deal to art.

'Cliff, darling,' she said as we embraced. 'I've longed for this day.'

'Come off it, Rube.' I slapped her ample rump. 'This is a business call.'

She laughed. 'What else, you old bastard. There was a time when I thought you might take off your trench coat and have a little fun.'

'I've never worn a trench coat in my life, and just now I'm having all the fun I need, thanks very much.'

'Amateurs,' she said as she subsided into a chair. 'Okay, waste some of my time.'

I sat and felt the soft padding ooze around me. I could almost sense the many gentlemen's trousers that had been draped over the chair.

'I'm looking for a working girl, Rube, but my last piece of information goes back over twenty years.'

While she's no saint and has played very rough in her time, Ruby has genuine concern for the people she employs and others in the sex business. She shook her head sadly. 'Not many survive that long, mate.'

'I know it's a long shot. This woman's name was Pixie Padrone. I thought you—'

Ruby sat bolt upright, her upholstered breasts heaving. 'Pixie, that bitch!'

'You know her?'

'I should. She was on the street like you say, a real low-life. Asked me for a spot but she was a hopeless junkie and she'd had more claps than a symphony orchestra. Then all of a sudden she's cleaned up her act. She's off the shit and working out of a flash flat in Point Piper. She took away some of my business for a while and didn't she rub my nose in it.'

'When was this?'

'Like you say, at least twenty years ago.'

'I mean specifically.'

'Shit, Cliff, it's a long time ago.'

'I'm talking about 1983.'

She thought, then shook her head. 'No, must've been a year or so later. I was in Enzed for most of eighty-three— avoiding a couple of warrants. I put in a manager here.'

'You didn't know her brother killed a doctor in Darlinghurst?'

'I might've heard something about it when I got back, but I didn't pay it much attention. There was a lot going on thereabouts, what with the AIDS thing hitting and all that.'

'When you say she'd cleaned up her act, what d'you mean exactly, Rube?'

'Jesus, you're really into exactly and specifically and precisely, aren't you?'

''fraid so, it's like that.'

'I mean that she must've gone to some detox place and got herself cleaned out. Takes time and money, that. Plus, she'd had her teeth fixed, boob job, the works.'

'Where is she now?'

'Haven't a clue. She took off somewhere with her pimp. Funny, you saying her brother killed a doctor. Pixie's bloke was supposed to be a doctor. Probably an abortionist.'

'What was his name?'

'Can't remember. Adolf, Boris—something German like.'

9

I pressed Ruby for more information about Pixie Padrone but she'd run dry. According to her, Pixie vanished from the Sydney sex scene 'sometime around when Australia won the America's Cup', which was as close as she could pin it down.

'That was a boom time, if you like,' she said. 'I wish they'd bung on stuff like that permanently.'

She said she'd ask around about Pixie, but she didn't hold out much hope.

'She must have had parents, family of some kind apart from her brother?'

'If Pixie had parents,' Ruby said, 'they probably kicked her out before she got her first period. She was a grade one troublemaking bitch.'

In a perverse way, that was a ringing endorsement from Ruby, who has a low opinion of humankind in general, and women in particular. For Pixie to be worthy of such an assessment, she had to be a person of some force. I thanked Ruby and promised to introduce her after I'd told her about Lily.

'I need someone to write my autobiography, Cliff,' Ruby said. 'Journalists do that sort of thing, don't they?'

'They do. Not sure Lily would. She's more on the financial side.'

'Shit, you think I'm not financial? I get all sorts of tips from the market high-flyers and do bloody well out of them. Your girlfriend'd be surprised about the financial stuff that goes on here, and the money side of this business.'

'I'll talk to her,' I said. 'What about dinner at the Bourbon and Beefsteak? On me?'

'You're on. I could go a chateaubriand. Make it a night early in the week.'

My day's work had given me plenty to think about—connections that could be important, possible survivors to seek out, questions needing answers. I drove to my office in Newtown to do the thinking and the computer work if that seemed likely to be helpful. The office is two floors up in a building at the non-trendy end of King Street. The creeping gentrification that has transformed Newtown seems to have stalled at the moment, but no doubt it'll get on the move again, like the cane toad up north.

Before going to the office I collected my mail from the post office box and, as usual, was able to dispose of a good deal of it in a street bin. The bills were accumulating as they do, but there was a decent cheque as well to help things along. Bpay had taken some of the nuisance and expense out of paying accounts, but the equation was just the same. What was coming in versus what was going out. So far this year, with about a third of it gone, I was holding my own. That was good going, because summer and spring are bad for business generally. Things pick up in winter when people tend to have darker, more suspicious thoughts.

The office is conducive to thinking—spartan, functional, with the coffee maker as the only comfort item since the bar fridge went on the blink. I booted up the computer and wrote down as many of the words spoken by all parties in the interviews as I could remember. This is a new technique for me, as advised by Lily. She says that exact, direct quotes can sometimes get you to the heart of the matter. Hasn't happened yet, but it might. For Lil, the words on the screen are totally real. Me, I need to print things out to get the feel.

I spent the rest of the afternoon going over what I'd written together with Frank's extensive notes, trying to piece things together. If Dr Karl Lubeck was associated with Rafael Padrone's sister, then the removal of his medical file was unlikely to be an accident—incidental to the removal of incriminating material—as Roma Brown had thought. If Pixie Padrone had pulled herself out of addiction through expensive detoxification treatment and had had some bodywork, again expensive, that suggested she'd got her hands on some money. Maybe some of her brother's twenty thousand?

But what light, if any, did this throw on the possibility of Gregory Heysen being innocent of conspiracy to murder Peter Bellamy? My one thought to date was that Heysen could have been framed as a consequence of something going wrong in the clandestine makeover racket. Not easy to investigate, let alone prove. But there was another connection, confirming Ruby's linking of Pixie with someone with a German name said to be a doctor and, therefore, possibly Lubeck—plastic surgery.

It felt like progress, but of a very cobwebbed kind, not something to report back to Frank on. I checked on the

America's Cup victory—1983—with Hawkie calling any employer who'd docked a worker's wages for taking a day off 'a bum'. Hawke and Bond, two fallen heroes. Give or take a bit, that date fitted in with Karl Lubeck, having dropped Roma Brown, operating as Pixie Padrone's pimp. And it firmed up the likelihood that she had got her hands on a useful sum of money for her rehabilitation.

Not wanting to get distracted from the Heysen matter, I'd left checking my email until I got home. The rain had stopped but I wasn't in the mood to deal with the fallen branch, and aluminium ladders don't rust. I made myself a gin and tonic and hit the keys. There was a scattering of spam as usual—offers to lengthen my penis, harden it and make it more responsive. Delete, delete, delete, though the day may come.

My accountant wanted me to send in my quarterly tax stuff, and my annual dues for the Balmain Rugby League Club, my one such membership, were overdue. The only message of interest was from my daughter, Megan, who was on a cruise ship in the Pacific providing nightly entertainment in the form of a two-hander song and dance show. Her partner was one Daniel Wilson-Fox and they were apparently an item:

Hi Cliff. Danny and I are wowing 'em here on the boat. It's a good gig and we're saving money. Did you know that old women dye their hair blue because it looks yellow to them because their eyesight is shot? Thought that might be helpful professionally.
Love
Megan

I couldn't see how, but it was nice to get the message. I sent a quick reply and felt glad that Megan had life by the scruff. I'd been lucky; all her major troubles happened before I even knew she existed. And ever since I'd helped her out of the aftermath of them we'd got on well. That returned me to thoughts of William Heysen, who may or may not have been Frank Parker's son, and who I was supposed to find. Hadn't put in any time on that as yet.

I went up to the Toxteth Hotel for a meal, a few drinks and a couple of games of pool. I teamed up with Daphne Rowley, a regular, and we held the table for a while against a succession of young bloods. Always a good feeling.

On Saturday morning I got up early and bought the papers, skimmed them, and went to the gym. I sometimes get good ideas on the treadmill where the activity is so boring the brain is forced to make a contribution to help the time pass. I set it at the moderate pace for the first ten minutes and then lifted it for the next twenty. The machine is set to stop after thirty minutes to prevent people from hogging it, simulating a City to Surf run. I built the grade up gradually but not too far, out of consideration for my hamstrings.

An aerobics class was going on in an adjoining room with the appropriate music pumping out at high decibels. Preferable to the inane commercial radio station that occasionally pollutes the air until someone complains. I blank the music out and concentrate on finding a rhythm. I broke into a light sweat, which is about the time the ideas come. It's nothing to do with endorphins because by then I'm feeling the pain.

I ran the case over in my mind, recalling the conversations as I'd written them up and the connections and associations. I sweated, but nothing came except the renewed conviction that Pixie Padrone and Karl Lubeck felt like the keys to the whole affair. Neither of them was old. To judge by Roma Brown's account, Lubeck was in good health, and when last heard of Pixie was in the pink. They should both still be alive, but where? With sweat running into my eyes I looked up at the bank of television sets I usually ignore. One was tuned to CNN and George W Bush was stumbling through a speech. I hoped to hell they hadn't gone to America.

I got home with that depressing thought in mind but my mood lifted immediately when I found that Lil was back. We had a shower together and went to bed for the afternoon—sex, sleep, more sex and more sleep. Come evening and we went to the Taste of India in Glebe Point Road for dinner. A pleasant stroll, well rugged up against the cool night air, wine from the Ancient Briton across the road, Glebe at its best.

The waiters know us and know we don't like fuss and dislike having our wine poured for us. We were both hungry and ate steadily for a while before talking about our work. I filled Lily in on what I'd done and how things looked.

'Early days,' she said.

'Yeah, but the longer it takes the more it costs Frank.'

'He can afford it, can't he?'

'I suppose so, but he had to conceal it from Hilde, which he hates doing, and I feel the same. Anyway, that's me. How's the MFP?'

She snapped a pappadum in half. 'Don't ask.'

'That bad?'

'Worse. I'll be battling to get any juice into it.'

'You will.'

We ate and drank a bit more and I was thinking about asking for our second bottle—we were walking home, after all—when Lily said, 'I've been considering what you've told me, Cliff. I know you, you're a bit stymied, right?'

I told her about the treadmill session, making a joke of it.

'Masochist,' she said, putting her fork down. 'But it sounds as though this Lubeck could be a plastic surgeon, right?'

'Could be, but probably a fly-by-nighter.'

'Exactly. I did a piece on dodgy plastic surgeons a year or so ago. Before I met you.'

'I wonder that you could have any memory of such a desolate time in your life.'

'Piss off. This bloke was full bottle on that scene. He's a real sleaze. I could hardly bear to talk to him and the thought of him touching me made my skin crawl. But if your bloke's working in that area anywhere in Australia, Norman Belfrage will know about him.'

'*Doctor* Belfrage?'

Lil picked up her fork. 'Was once,' she said. 'Don't open the other bottle, Cliff. I have to work tomorrow.'

10

Lil spent Sunday on the computer and the phone. I went for a long morning walk through Glebe and Annandale and rewarded myself with a beer at the Toxteth. I flicked through the papers without reading anything of interest and did a couple of crosswords, trying to tell myself this was valuable down time, restorative. I wasn't convinced; I wanted to be up and running.

Around 7 pm I took a glass of wine up to Lil and told her I was putting together one of my culinary specialities— a mixed grill.

'Thanks,' she said. 'I'll be down in a few minutes. Don't burn the bangers.'

Over the meal she told me she'd contacted the man she called Nasty Norman and that he'd agreed to meet me.

'For a consideration, I assume?'

'Right. I got him down to five hundred dollars for an hour, plus a bottle of brandy.'

'Thanks, Lil. When?'

'Tomorrow, eleven o'clock, at the Newport Workers Club. He's a ratty little number with a bad comb-over. He's got emphysema but he'll be smoking. Sometimes it takes him five minutes to get enough breath for a sentence.'

'Sounds lovely. Good way to start the week.'

'At least you'll be out and about. I'll still be trying to pump some life into this turkey of a story.'

I poured us both some more wine and used the bit of sausage I'd kept aside to mop up the Rosella. 'Do you have a copy of the piece you wrote on dicey plastic surgery?'

'It's on the thumb drive. I'll print you a copy. The subs butchered it, of course. Won't tell you much.'

'Anything'll be a lot compared to what I know now.'

Lil went back to work. Before starting she printed out her article. I stacked the dishes—very few from a minimalist cook like me—and settled down with the article and the last of the red we'd had with dinner. If Lil was having difficulty getting the MFP story up and running, she'd had no trouble with this one. She captured the rapacious, unscrupulous character of the doctors who did plastic surgery on the cheap and without proper referrals or investigation of the backgrounds of their 'clients'.

Their usual habit was to get people going under the knife to sign waivers exempting the surgeons from responsibility for outcomes. It was amazing how many desperate people –some young and seeking to change their fortunes, some older, trying to recapture their youth—were prepared to do this. Lil implied that some of the surgery was to change appearance to avoid arrest, or re-arrest. No names, no pack drill, but at least one of the dodgy doctors had been tied in with a passport-forging enterprise that had gone wrong and put all parties behind bars. The doctor in question, who carried the nickname 'the cutter', had received the lightest sentence for his cooperation with the authorities, but he hadn't survived six months inside the gaol.

Lil finished working and came down the stairs yawning. She leaned over me as I jotted down some notes illegible to anyone else, and sometimes to me.

'It's a great piece,' I said. 'Should've got a Walkley.'

'That's my ambition. What d'you think I'm hanging around with you for?'

Time was when Newport was fairly unfashionable and fairly affordable. Not now. Never mind that salt air rusts the guttering and zaps the computers, Sydney people want to be as close to the water as they can. Plenty of money had been spent in Newport since I'd last been there. The old houses had just about disappeared to make way for apartment blocks and the ones that had survived had been renovated and modified so that their original owners wouldn't have known them.

The Workers Club was at the south end of Newport beach with a view straight out over the Tasman Sea or the Pacific Ocean, take your pick. I'd stopped in Dee Why to pick up the brandy. I don't drink the stuff unless there's nothing else around, and don't know one brand from another. Hennessy appealed to my Irish ancestry.

The club building had undergone change like everything else around, and not necessarily for the better. It had that generic look of polished metal and glass, potted plants and photographs of club officials with chins spilling down towards their tie knots. In my slip-ons, clean jeans, blue shirt and blazer, I passed the dress regulations comfortably. The club was affiliated with almost every other club in the state, so my Balmain membership got me full privileges, whatever they were.

The addicts were feeding the pokies, the alkies were nursing their drinks, and the old surfers were staring out at the rolling waves. The thing about Sydney beaches is that they have a way of looking good whatever the weather. This Monday morning was one that might go this way or that as it developed. There was a mild southerly, good waves, but dark cloud building.

I was early, a chronic habit. I bought a middy of light and sat at a table where I could see the entrance and keep an eye on the water. I'd surfed here myself in days gone by, but preferred the southern beaches.

He came in at eleven-twenty. Lil's description had been accurate and he was easy to spot. After climbing the few steps he was out of breath and clutched the metal handrail as a spasm of coughing seized him. He survived it and lit a cigarette the instant it passed.

He wore a tweed jacket that had seen much better days and he took it off slowly as he looked around. I stood and he moved towards me, folding his coat over his arm in an oddly old-world gesture. He was dressed in a grey pullover, cream shirt and grey slacks, the jumper and pants streaked with cigarette ash.

He approached the table and looked at me with eyes that had a milkiness suggesting cataracts forming.

'Mr Belfrage,' I said.

'Doctor Belfrage, if you please.'

'What'll you have, doctor?'

He lowered himself into a chair. 'I'll have a middy of black and a large brandy.'

I bought the drinks and when I got back he'd lined up a packet of fifty cigarettes and his lighter, and drawn the ashtray closer. He accepted the drinks without thanks, took a sizeable sip of the brandy and a long pull on the middy after inhaling smoke. He exhaled and leaned back in the chair letting the drugs do their work. The area we were in was quiet but activity was beginning in the cafeteria adjacent, and further off the pokies were whirring.

'Private investigator, eh?' he said. 'I used to employ blokes like you when my clients didn't pay up. Do much of that sort of work?'

'Not much.'

'I hope you brought the brandy.'

I lifted the bottle in its paper bag from the chair beside me. 'Hennessy,' I said. 'Hope that's all right.'

He went through the smoke-inhaling drink-absorbing ritual again. 'It'll do. What d'you want to know?'

'Do you remember a doctor named Bellamy being murdered and his partner, Heysen, being convicted of conspiring to kill him?'

'Vaguely.'

'I've been told Heysen and another doctor were performing illicit plastic surgery.'

'In what sense illicit?'

'I mean clandestine and for people wanting to change their appearance for other than cosmetic reasons.'

'Nicely put. Well it happened, certainly.'

'But you can't confirm it in this case.'

'It's a long time ago. Your lady friend traduced me, you know.'

It was clear he was going to play a very cautious game with diversionary tactics.

He smoked and drank some more and looked around as if he'd lost interest in the conversation. His skin was grey and drawn tight over the bones of his face. His greasy, dun-coloured hair was plastered across his skull like a smear of mud. His hands, one holding the cigarette, the other wrapped around a glass, were thin with long fingers and bloodless nails. Lily was right—you wouldn't want him to touch you.

I decided to be direct. 'I'll try a name on you—Dr Karl Lubeck,' I said. 'Have you heard of him?'

He looked at me with the milky eyes. 'Yes, he worked with Heysen in Darlinghurst.'

'So you do remember about Heysen's sideline?'

'I do, and I can probably remember a deal more if I see the money and . . .' he tossed off the rest of the brandy and beer, 'I get another drink. Same again.'

This time when I came back a garishly dressed old crone with a corrugated face was standing next to Belfrage, who was lighting the cigarette she'd obviously bludged.

'Give Dulce a few dollars, Hardy, so she can dream of a jackpot.'

I handed the woman some change and she mooched away.

'One of your clients, doctor?' I said.

'Watch your mouth.'

'I'm getting sick of this, Belfrage. I know what a defrocked, discredited, dis-fucking-grace to your profession you are. I've got the money and you can have it if you tell me something useful. Otherwise you can sink those two drinks and fuck off without the money or the brandy.'

He sat very still and lit another cigarette. 'Don't smoke, do you?'

'Not anymore.'

'How did you stop?'

'Stubbornness.'

'Yes, I can believe that. What do you want to know about Karl?'

'Where he and a woman named Pixie Padrone are.'

'Pixie!' He tried to drink and laugh at the same time and was overwhelmed by a coughing fit that shook him from head to toe. The cigarette fell from his fingers and the brandy glass hit the table, slopping out half of its contents. I put the cigarette in the ashtray and pushed the middy towards him as he fought for breath. After he managed to suck in a few wheezy gasps he drank some beer and reached for the cigarette. People were staring at us. I gripped his bony wrist, trying to look solicitous.

'Breathe some air and tell me about it.'

His puny chest heaved as air flowed into his wrecked system. 'You shouldn't make me laugh. You'll kill me.'

'Karl and Pixie, where?'

He wrapped both hands around the middy glass like a drowning man clutching at driftwood. 'Pixie Padrone, I remember when she was that. She could be had for ten dollars, five on a slow night. Now she's Patricia.'

'Okay. Take it slowly, I don't want you dropping dead quite yet. Tell me about them, especially where they are.'

'Brisbane.'

'I couldn't find him in the medical registry. Has he been delisted, like you?'

'You're trying to provoke me. No, he's changed his name. He's Karol Lubitsch now and, as I said, Pixie is Patricia.'

'Where in Brisbane?'

'They have a clinic in New Farm, Glendale Gardens or some such pretentious address.'

I moved around the table and put the bottle of brandy on the seat next to him.

'The money?' he said.

'In a minute. How would you suggest I get to see Lubeck . . . Lubitsch?'

The cloudy eyes studied me again. 'How many times has that nose been broken?'

'Several.'

'And the scarred eyebrows—boxing, I take it?'

'Right.'

'The nose could be remodelled and scars smoothed out. I'd suggest you get a referral from a doctor. A man in your trade should have a tame medico.'

'I wouldn't call him tame, but it can be done. Good idea.'

He snapped the long, blue-white fingers. 'So?'

'I've got just one problem. What's to stop you contacting Lubitsch and alerting him that I'm coming?'

He lit a cigarette from the butt of the previous one and drew on it with a surprising amount of wind. 'Why would I do that?'

'To bleed money from him, of course.'

He held up his hand. 'Don't make me laugh again. There's no love lost between Karol Lubitsch and me, I assure you. We had a serious falling out long ago. I passed a client to him who gave him a considerable amount of trouble. Legal trouble, which is what everyone in the profession fears most.'

'I can imagine.'

'At a guess, it's the same for you. I wouldn't want Lubitsch to know where I am or what I'm doing. He'd almost certainly take reprisals. And I'm sure you mean him harm, which is fine by me.' He ran out of breath for speaking but not for smoking, as if the nicotine opened some air passages. 'Malice, Mr Hardy,' he wheezed, 'is my middle name.'

I believed him and handed over the money.

11

'How did it go?' Lily asked.

I'd dropped in at a post office on the way home and checked the Brisbane telephone directory. Dr Karl Lubitsch's address was listed as suites 12–14, Glendale Gardens, New Farm.

'You were right on all counts,' I said. 'He's an absolute creep, but he came through with the information I wanted. By the way, he said you traduced him.'

'Bullshit, I changed the name. So where are they?'

'Brisbane.'

'Uh oh, off again. Pretty soon we'll be meeting in airports.'

'Or joining the mile high club.'

'You wish. Well, it'll be warmer up there and I'll have the place here to myself to work.'

'There's a storm brewing. Phone the NRMA insurance if the roof blows off. Is it hard to get to see these guys?'

'Not for the initial consultation . . . What're you talking about?'

'I'm going to pretend to be a patient.'

'Client, please.'

*

Ian Sangster has been my doctor through metres of stitches and bandage and kilos of plaster of Paris. He laughed like a drain when I told him what I wanted. 'You know what happened to Harry Grebb?'

I did. Grebb, world light-heavyweight champion in the twenties and the only man ever to beat Gene Tunney, had died under the anaesthetic during an operation to straighten his pugilistic hooter.

'Don't worry, I won't be going under the knife.'

'You could do with a bit.'

'The closest I've ever come to cosmetic surgery is getting circumcised and I didn't have a say.'

I gave him the details and he said I could pick up the referral later in the day. I phoned the Brisbane number. A cool-voiced female receptionist answered. I told her I had a referral to Dr Lubitsch, and asked how soon I could see him.

'Would Friday suit you?'

'Nothing before that?'

'I'm afraid not. Unless there's a cancellation. What kind of medical cover do you have?'

'Top rank Medibank Private.'

She took down my number and said she'd phone if there was a cancellation. She rang back within an hour to say I could have an appointment at 8.30 am on Wednesday. I accepted.

'Please have your referral and your Medibank Private card with you.'

'Am I supposed to fast or bring a urine sample?'

She giggled. 'No, nothing like that. The initial consultation is more of a chat.'

'Wonder what you'll pay for a chat,' Lily said when

I told her I'd booked on a Tuesday afternoon Virgin flight to Brisbane in order to make the early Wednesday slot.

'That's a point. I'm going through Frank's money at a rate of knots.'

'Maybe you can get some more from the winsome widow.'

'All I can tell her is that her kid made a good impression on a bloke in a profession she despises. Not something she's likely to want to hear. Oh, and that her late hubby did hush-hush plastic surgery.'

As soon as I spoke, the thought struck me that Catherine Heysen was on a wild goose chase. If I could prove that her husband hadn't organised his partner's murder, still very problematical, it would most likely involve his work as a dodgy plastic surgeon. That was a revision hardly likely to divert the son onto the straight and narrow path. It felt like something to talk over with Frank. Although I hadn't wanted to give him an update yet, I decided I'd better.

'I'm free,' he said when I rang him.

'How about an overpriced drink out at the airport around one o'clock?'

'You're on.'

'What'll you tell Hilde?'

'Not your problem. See you there.'

I didn't like the sound of that but he was right. I had enough problems, including the major one of what I was going to say or do when I came face to face with Dr Karol Lubitsch, aka Karl Lubeck.

I put the Falcon in the long-term parking area, checked my one bag in the required time ahead of the flight, and passed through the metal detectors without setting off any bells and whistles. I had an old sports bag containing a book, a newspaper folded to the crossword page, a map of Brisbane and environs and a collapsible umbrella. I'd checked the weather and found it was going to be ten degrees warmer in Brisbane than in Sydney, but with storms threatening.

Frank was sitting at a table staring out at the planes on the tarmac and nursing a beer. He looked as though he wished he could get on one of the planes and head off. I bought a drink and took a seat opposite him.

'Why here?' he said.

'My investigation on your behalf is taking me to Brisbane.'

'Half your luck.'

I had no option but to tell him what I'd been doing and the way things were looking at that point. He seemed disappointed that I hadn't put in any time on finding William Heysen.

'That wasn't my brief.'

'Yeah, sorry. My mind has been running on him a bit.'

I made the point I had to make—that, however it came out, young Heysen wasn't going to see his father as a model citizen and change his ways.

He nodded as if he'd come to the same conclusion himself before I even spoke. I was worried about him. Always spare, he'd lost weight and the lines on his face were more deeply etched. He was jumpy, wired. He finished his beer, got up and brought back two more.

'It might all take a different turn, mate,' he said.

'How's that?'

'Hilde knows something's wrong. She reads me like a book. I think I'm going to have to come clean about it all.'

'Could be the best thing.'

'Yeah, except she's in this funny state and there's a complication. We haven't heard from Peter in a while and there're reports of trouble in the part of South America he's in. She's very worried about him and I am, too. Not exactly the best time to spring a problem love child on her.'

'How serious are the reports? How credible?'

Frank shrugged. 'I don't know. I'm trying to find out more but the place isn't exactly well-ordered. He's looking into logging near the border of Brazil and Colombia. Hard to know what to believe.'

'What did you mean about things taking a different turn?'

Frank blinked, as though he was looking into the future and couldn't hold his gaze steady. 'God knows how Hilde'll react when I spell it out for her. Then there's Catherine. She's likely to want a DNA test to confirm I'm her son's father. She says she's got hair samples. If I *am* the father . . .'

'What?'

'I'd have to do something about straightening him out myself.'

I started on the second drink, hardly realising that I'd downed the first. 'Jesus, Frank, that'd be getting into deep water.'

His smile was humourless. 'With undertow.'

'Maybe we should just chuck the whole thing about Heysen. He was bent in one way or another. What's the difference?'

'No. Something went wrong in that investigation. I'd at least like to see that straightened out, even if everything else goes to hell in a hand cart.'

I wondered about his thinking. Was he still so attracted to Catherine Heysen that he'd consider trading one woman and one son for another woman and another son? Unlikely, but men in chaos think chaotically and do chaotic things.

Frank watched me as I chewed over what he'd said. Out of habit I felt for the boarding pass in my jacket pocket and he misinterpreted the movement. Before I could stop him he'd pulled out a cheque book and was writing.

'No, Frank.'

He ripped the cheque out, tearing a corner. 'What the hell. I'm going to see this through whatever it takes. You've paid Wain and Belfrage, right?'

'Yes, a bit, but—'

He shoved the cheque into my shirt pocket. 'Plane fare, accommodation, car hire, it all costs. I can afford it, Cliff.'

'What about Hilde and the cheque account?'

He sank his beer and got up. 'I'm going to tell her the whole story when I get home. Good luck, mate. Take care of yourself.'

Budget flying is okay for short trips but I prefer business class with the majors when a well-heeled client is paying. I wasn't going to load the expense account for Frank, but I found he'd given me a cheque for five thousand, which was over the top. He'd been jumpy, thirsty, distracted, nothing like the Frank I knew. I hoped he wasn't headed for a crisis of some kind. He'd handled plenty of professional crises in his time, but personal ones involving family are a different matter.

The plane battled against headwinds all the way and ran into heavy turbulence over the Gold Coast. The sideways lurches and stomach-dropping free-falls matched my pessimistic mood. I was by the window and had given up on Anna Funder's *Stasiland*, fascinating though it was, because I couldn't keep the book steady enough to read. When I saw lightning flashes not too far away I began to get that this-could-be-it feeling. I've had it before. I wouldn't say your life flashes before your eyes but, in my case, I do tend to conduct a bit of a life review along 'I did it my way' lines. It stops the instant of touchdown.

As predicted, the air was steamy in Brisbane, as if the whole city was waiting for the storm cell to reach it and break. Despite the heat, everyone was hurrying to go about their business, and I could feel the tension around the carousel as we waited for our bags. Seemed like a hundred mobile phones were glued to a hundred ears. My bag came off early, and I beat some competitors to the Avis desk where I hired a Pulsar.

I drove out of the airport, which they've had the sense to locate at a distance from the city, under a sky the colour of bruised blood plums. I'd booked into the closest motel I could find to Glendale Gardens, in Brunswick Street, New Farm—a good spot near some shops and cheap in the off season. I was on the second level looking down towards the river. I'd unpacked my bag and cracked a Fourex from the mini-bar when the storm hit. Had I wound up the window on the Pulsar? I hoped so, but I certainly wasn't going down to check in this. The hail came first, golfball-sized, pelting the roof and the small balcony but melting immediately on the warm surfaces. The rain followed. It lashed down, driven by a stiff wind that bent the trees, shredding the ones with leaves.

Dry and warm with a drink in hand, a storm is a bit of pleasant drama to watch. Not so much fun if you're out in it as I have been plenty of times. The gutters ran, filled, overflowed and water washed across the roads. The few cars still moving threw up skeins of water, bonnet and roof high. Thunderclaps shook the building, or seemed to, and the lightning flashes flickered and darted across the sky like artillery.

A knock came at the door and I tore myself away from the show to answer it. The very gay young man who'd checked me in was standing damply with his umbrella half open.

'Oh, Mr Hardy, just checking. Did any water come in through the balcony door?'

'Not a drop.'

'Good, good. Luckily, you're on the right side of the building, but just making sure. One of the other rooms is awash.'

'Pretty dramatic, isn't it?'

'I suppose so. Your satellite TV reception could be out for a while. Hope you weren't watching the cricket.'

'Never do.'

'Really? You look like a sportsman.'

'Boxing.'

'Oh, well, glad everything's all right.'

I went back to the window, and as quickly as it had arrived, the storm passed. The clouds rolled back and the sun shone through, producing a rainbow and causing steam to rise from the wet roads. All in all, it was one of the best receptions I'd ever had on arriving anywhere. I drained the can and scored a hit in the wpb. Good start.

When the sky was totally clear I grabbed the umbrella and went for a walk down Brunswick Street, past the shops and on to the park that ran alongside the river. It was a nice

park—big, not fussy and with plenty of Moreton Bay figs,
the way a Brisbane park should be. There was a wide cycle
and walking path around the perimeter that probably ran
for close on two kilometres and the walkers and joggers
and cyclists and rollerbladers were out already, splash-
ing through the patchy shallow puddles and squelching
through the thick layer of leaves blown down by the storm.
A woman in running gear pushing a pram was moving
along at a fast clip, passing the slowcoaches.

I'd more or less memorised the map and found my way
to Glendale Gardens easily enough. The street was up-
market—apartment blocks interspersed with big houses
and a couple of high-rent commercial buildings. The
Lubitsch place was in one these—a pale blue structure,
three storeys, set at the highest point of the street. The front
suites on the second and third levels would have a nice view
out over the park and the river. Lubitsch was in suites 12 to
14 and it was a fair bet that he'd be up there in front. When
you're at a prestige address you want the best position.

I walked back to the motel, stopping to buy a bottle of
wine and check out the eateries. Plenty to choose from. I'd
been hoping the walk would give me some idea of how to
tackle Lubitsch, but nothing came. Except this: he was
obviously doing well, had acquired a lot, and while that can
be a plus it can also be a minus because what you've got you
don't want to lose.

12

I 'd given Frank the phone number of the motel and he rang me when I got back from dinner.

'Got you,' he said. 'I've been trying for a while.'

'What's up?'

'Have you got any grog to hand? As if I need to ask.'

I had a third of the bottle of white wine left from my meal at a Spanish joint. 'Yes,' I said.

'Pour it.'

I did. 'Hate to say it, Frank, but you sound a bit pissed.'

'I am, Hilde is as well. We're well into our second bottle of champagne and thinking about a third. Peter's been in touch.'

I had a drink. 'That's good.'

'He's in love.'

'That's better.'

'Yeah, and his girlfriend's pregnant with twins. Hilde's over the moon. They're coming back soon. Shit, I'm rhyming. I *am* pissed.'

'That's great news. When did this happen?'

'Hilde told me when I got back from meeting you. Then Peter phoned again.'

'I see. And have you . . .?'

'Of course I have. Hilde was afraid I was hiding cancer from her or something. She's relieved and she's fine about it. I mean about the boy possibly being mine. She says I should find out for sure.'

Yeah, I thought, and what about your attraction to Catherine Heysen? But I said: 'What effect does all this have on the investigation?'

'I haven't thought it through yet, but I want you to go on. If Heysen was railroaded I was partly responsible and I'd like that cleared up. I owe it to the kid whoever's son he is.'

'And if he's yours you'll want to help him get out of the shitty business he says he's in.'

'That's right, and the same goes if he isn't. We'll cross that bridge when we come to it.'

Frank didn't usually speak in cliches and his voice was slurring. He put Hilde on the line and I made all the right noises. Too many times I'd had to tell a person someone they loved was dead. At those moments the misery fills the air like a mist. This was the opposite and, through the wine and the remains of her German accent, I could hear happiness in every word Hilde spoke.

That left me alone in a motel room with two-thirds of a bottle of wine inside me and garlic on my breath. I stripped and had a warm shower followed by a cold one. I cleaned my teeth till my gums ached, made a cup of instant coffee and settled down with *Stasiland*. I was tempted to ring Lily, but that wasn't the deal.

I presented myself at the Lubitsch clinic dead on time— shaved, shampooed, neatly dressed and with my documents in hand. The giggling receptionist was a youngish blonde with a lively manner. She was good to look at, had a pleasant voice and was adept at putting people at their ease. Handy talent. She gave me a form to fill in and I did it with a mixture of fact and fiction. I gave my profession as security consultant, owned up to a few minor operations, mostly to repair injuries, and ticked the 'facial' box in the question about 'areas of concern'. I wrote truthfully that I was a non-smoker but less truthfully that my drinking was limited to 'occasional social'.

The receptionist looked the form over and gave me one of her toothpaste advertisement smiles. 'Dr Lubitsch will see you in a few minutes, Mr Hardy.'

I nodded and sat in a chair that allowed me to look out a window. She went away with the form and came back quickly to resume her place behind the desk where she must have been doing something though it was hard to tell what it might have been. As I'd suspected, the clinic was on the top level and the view was all I thought it would be. I picked up a couple of the magazines from the rack, but the view was more interesting. I got an eyeful of the river and watched one of the big passenger catamarans churn past. A buzzer sounded and the receptionist stood.

'This way please, Mr Hardy.'

I followed her down a passage. She knocked at a door, pushed it open and ushered me in. The room was large and light, probably one of the largest and lightest in the building. Its occupant was sitting behind a big steel and glass desk, studying my form. He half stood, then sat down heavily in his leather chair and gestured with his head for me to take the other chair.

I'd decided on a direct approach. I ignored his instruction, locked the door behind me and went to his desk.

I flicked the off switch on the intercom and disconnected the phone. He rose and I pushed him down hard. Lubitsch may have been a big man twenty-odd years ago when Roma Brown knew him briefly, but he'd shrunk vertically and expanded horizontally. He was twenty kilos overweight and his belly pushed out his spotless clinician's coat. He wore a crisp white shirt under it with a dark tie and dark trousers. He was bald, apart from grey fluff around the sides, but at least he hadn't committed the Belfrage-style comb-over.

'What the hell d'you think you're doing? You must be mad.' He reached for the switch on the intercom and I rabbit-chopped his wrist.

'Shut up, sit still and listen and you won't get hurt.'

'What do you want? There's no money here.'

'I said listen.'

I told him that I knew he was Karl Lubeck and that he'd worked doing illicit plastic surgery with a Dr Gregory Heysen who'd been jailed for conspiracy to commit murder. Also that he'd taken files from the doctor's office to conceal their activities. And that he'd subsequently profited from the money that had been paid to the murderer of Dr Peter Bellamy before becoming the pimp for a woman named Pixie Padrone.

He was already pasty-faced from spending too much time indoors, but he went still paler. Had a shot at bluffing, though.

'Preposterous,' he said.

I took a camera from my pocket, raised it and took a photo of him there in his chair with the fear in his eyes and his mouth slack.

'What . . . what's that for?'

I studied the image on the screen and nodded. 'Pretty

good. The media'll want a picture when I tell them what I've just told you and provide proof.'

I looked around the room with its black filing cabinets, bar fridge, teak bookshelf, framed degrees, photographs and paintings. 'You can kiss goodbye to all this, unless . . .'

He sighed but seemed to recover some poise. 'How much?'

It seemed too quick and too easy a surrender, and I remembered Belfrage saying that Lubitsch would take reprisals. It wouldn't do to underestimate him, flabby though he was. He'd come a long way and showed resourcefulness. But maybe his best days were behind him.

'I don't want money, doctor.'

That's when the poise left him completely. He coughed and spluttered and his wan face turned red. He shuddered and fought for breath. His chest heaved and the soft flesh covering it shook like jelly. I know I can look threatening but this was something else. He was having a panic attack. I grabbed him, pulled his tie loose and popped the top button on his shirt getting the collar open. I pushed his head down between his knees.

'Stay there and breathe.'

I opened the bar fridge, got a bottle of mineral water, filled a glass and brought it to him. He was getting some air in painfully. I lifted his chin and gave him the glass.

'Sip it.'

He clutched the glass in shaking hands and did as he was told. The flush slowly faded from his fat face and his hands steadied. 'Who sent you?' he whispered.

'We can talk about that,' I said. 'When's your next appointment?'

He looked at his gold watch. 'In forty minutes.'

'That's long enough. Tell me if I'm right. You're still doing things you shouldn't and they don't always go right.'

He nodded and took a couple of gulps of the water.

'Okay, now that's the sort of thing I want to talk to you about. If you come up with the right answers I just might be able to put your mind at rest. No questions, just answers. Why did you take Michael Padrone's file along with the others?'

'Pixie . . . Patricia asked me to.'

'Why?'

'She said there were things in it that would make it worse for him.'

'How could things be worse? He'd confessed.'

'She said he'd done other things he'd told the doctor about and that if it came out he'd have a hellish time in prison for what little time he had left. Why are we talking about this?'

'I said no questions. What happened to the file?'

'She destroyed it and I destroyed the others.'

'Did Heysen have the same sort of problem you're facing—dissatisfied clients? Could one of them have framed Heysen? Hired Padrone to kill Bellamy and lie about who hired him?'

'Easily. I suspected so at the time, which is why I . . . made myself scarce.'

'Names.'

'It's a long time ago.'

'You don't forget people like that. Especially when you've cut into them. I want a list of names of possible candidates for what you just admitted could have happened. You're almost out of the woods, doctor.'

'What do you mean?'

'Get your gold pen out of your pocket and write.'

'I don't understand. This is twenty or more years ago.'

'You don't have to understand. You just have to write.'

'They're probably all dead.'

'That means you remember the names. Write.'

He took out his pen, pulled a pad towards him and scribbled.

I said. 'Capitals.'

He printed. I took a closer look at the things on the walls—expensive prints of paintings; degrees and diplomas, some American in the name of Lubitsch; photos of the doc when he was less fat with National Party politicians and a gaoled former police commissioner. One showed him standing proprietorially beside a slim blonde woman with a face stretched and frozen like Peggy Lee's. Her hands, holding a glass and her sequinned bag, were claw-like. Had to be Pixie.

'There.' He clicked the pen, tore off the sheet of paper and pushed it across the desk. I looked at it long enough to see that it was legible. One name jumped out at me but I didn't give him the satisfaction of reacting. I folded it and put it in my pocket.

'That's it,' I said.

'I don't understand.'

'You're repeating yourself. I'm not interested in anything you've done since the eighties. Your present problems are all your own as far as I'm concerned.'

'Can I believe that?'

'I couldn't care less. I would've liked to meet Pixie but I guess I'll just have to pass on that. You're going to be ready for your next victim. Might have to slip your tie up to look your best.'

'The photograph?'

'Insurance.'

He recovered fast. 'You bloody hoodlum. You threaten me . . .' His fleshy face took on a malevolent glow. 'In fact you could use my services.'

'Do you know what Marlon Brando said when Kenneth Tynan wanted to interview him? He said he'd rather be boiled in urine. That's how I feel about letting a plastic surgeon anywhere near me, especially you. Good morning, Dr Lubeck.'

'Get out!'

'I'm going. I'll give you one thing—remember Roma Brown?'

He did. He remembered it all.

'I didn't find you through her, by the way, but she did say you were good in bed. Doubt she'd think much of you now. Do you want me to give her your respects?'

The look on his face almost made me feel sorry for him. Almost. I suppose we all have regrets about old loves—missed opportunities, betrayals, yearnings, ecstatic moments that live in the memory. Lubitsch had been there, and I had a sense that things with Pixie/Patricia now weren't what he wanted. Good.

13

I walked back through the park, promising myself a jog there if I had time. I stopped for coffee in a kind of pavilion under the Moreton Bay figs and thought to myself that I'd done pretty well. I took the piece of paper from my shirt pocket and examined it. Three names, two completely unfamiliar to me. Inventions? I didn't think so, the man had been too frightened. The coffee was good and a light breeze was blowing pleasant smells around under the canvas. I had a second cup and took my time over it.

I paid, left a tip, skirted the cycle path and took another route past a shrubbery and garden bed towards the motel. A man stepped from the shadows and blocked my way. A big man, very big. He wore jeans and a leather jacket over a T-shirt and he tucked away a mobile phone as he confronted me.

'You've got something I want,' he said.

'What would that be?'

'A camera and a piece of paper.'

'Buy your own and look in a bin, you'll find plenty of paper.'

He advanced to within a yard and held out his right hand. 'Give.'

That was a mistake—an extended arm is vulnerable. I grabbed his wrist with both hands, jerked and twisted. He let out a yell and swung wildly at me with his left fist. He was no southpaw, the punch was slow and awkward. I stepped inside it and hammered my right fist into his ribs hard and twice. He grunted and bent over. He was game though and tried to do something with the arm I'd mistreated but it was all out of whack, possibly dislocated at the elbow, and his effort was feeble. I grabbed his right wrist again and put downward pressure on it. He almost screamed and sank to his knees to ease the strain and the pain.

He was young, fit-looking and strong but inexperienced. By now he was almost helpless and he knew it so he began to swear. I whacked him a backhander across the face and he stopped swearing.

'You tell Dr Lubitsch, or whoever he hired to hire you, that this sort of stuff is pretty much a full-time job with me. You weren't up to it.'

'Fuck you.'

'Grow up and learn your trade. If you'd held out your left hand you might've connected with your right and things could've gone your way, son. Give me your mobile.'

'What?'

'Give me your mobile or I'll break your jaw and scatter your teeth.'

He scrabbled in his jacket pocket for the phone and handed it to me.

'Right. Now you stay exactly where you are for ten minutes. I'll be able to see you, believe me. If you move, I'll chuck your phone in the river. If you behave it'll be waiting for you up at the exit to the park.'

I left him and walked away. They value their phones above all else for work and play, and I knew he'd do as I said. I didn't even have to look back. I put the phone on the sandstone gatepost and went on my way.

Sending a heavy after me, incompetent though he turned out to be, confirmed that the names Lubitsch had given me concerned him enough not to want to leave any evidence that he'd done so. I figured I'd done all I needed to do in Brisbane and it was time to go. There was just a chance that the doctor had other, better, helpers. Best to pass on the jog around the park. I booked on a mid-afternoon flight back to Sydney, willingly paid for the second night I wasn't going to spend in the motel and drove out to the airport. To judge by the windsocks, the wind was a southerly and should speed the flight home.

I was back in Glebe by late afternoon. Lily wasn't around and by agreement we hadn't got into the domestic habit of leaving notes about where we were and what we were doing. I was having a drink when Catherine Heysen rang.

'Mr Hardy, I suppose you've heard from Frank.'

'Yes.'

'He wants the DNA test.'

'I know. Are you going to have it done?'

'I'm not sure. Have you made any progress?'

'It's hard to say. I have some people to see and then I might have a better idea and be able to give you a report. I don't suppose you've heard from your son.'

'No, nothing.'

'Frank intends to help him, whether he's the father or not.'

Her voice softened, lost its arrogant edge. 'He's a fine man.'

Watch out, Frank, I thought, but I didn't say anything.

'If you need money, Mr Hardy . . .'

'Not at the moment and perhaps not at all. I'll be in touch, Mrs Heysen. Goodbye.'

As I put the phone down Lily came in carrying a pile of photocopies. 'Saw the car. That was quick.'

I kissed her. 'You know me—immediate results.'

She dumped the copies on a chair and gave me a hug. 'I've nearly finished this bastard. Hey, Hilde rang and wants us to come over for a bite. She knew you were in Brisbane, but now you're back, d'you want to go over there tonight? I could do with a break.'

'Sure. And I've got things to talk over with Frank. Did she tell you the news?'

'Did she what. Couldn't stop talking about it. I'll give her a ring. I must meet that kid of yours sometime.'

'Yeah. I'd like to see her again myself when she's ever in the one place long enough.'

'Who's she like, you or her mother?'

I thought of Megan's close physical resemblance to my sister and her restlessness, and my former wife's precise, planned approach to things. 'Me,' I said.

'God help her.'

After getting drunk out of relief and happiness the day before, Frank and Hilde had gone on a marathon bike ride and sweated out the toxins. From the way they were looking at each other I guessed they'd also had a good sexual workout or two. They were in fine form.

Hilde knocked up a barramundi dinner with all the trimmings and we got solidly into the dry white. Peter had sent a photo of his girlfriend electronically and they'd printed it out. It showed a vibrant, dark-skinned, raven-haired young woman smiling happily with pearly white teeth.

'Her name's Ramona,' Hilde said. 'She's Brazilian with Portuguese, African and Indian ancestry.'

'With Frank's English and your German background that should make for hybrid vigour. Are they going to live here?'

'Who knows with Peter?' Frank said. 'But they're getting married in Rio and coming here to have the babies.'

'I'll have to learn to cook Brazilian,' Hilde said.

'What does she do?' Lily asked.

Hilde laughed. 'Would you believe? She's a journalist.'

Hilde and Lily settled down to watch something on the History channel and Frank and I went to his study. I handed him Lubitsch's list.

'Let's see,' Frank said. 'Jesus Christ!'

The name that had struck me hit him just as hard: Matthew Henry Sawtell, known as 'Mad Matt'. He'd risen to the rank of detective inspector in the New South Wales police force and was tipped to go even higher when his world collapsed. An undercover sting operation showed him to be guilty of giving the green light to criminals, to sanctioning at least two murders and conspiring with a corrupt politician to fake a kidnapping with an outcome that would advantage them both.

'Mad Matt,' Frank said, almost whispering. 'Now he's a definite possibility. He escaped from Goulburn. Severely wounded a guard and killed an inmate. He was very high profile and nailing him was a big feather in the anti-corruption cap. Highly embarrassing for all concerned when he escaped. His file's still very much open although a lot of people would like it to be closed.'

'Meaning?'

'What d'you think? He had protection at a pretty high level until they just couldn't shield him anymore.'

'Did he put them in? I remember him going down but I forget the details.'

'No, he kept mum, but it doesn't take much to work out that he used those tickets when he needed to get out of gaol and away.'

'Nice town, Sawtell, up near Coffs. I surfed there when I was young. You knew him?'

Frank nodded. 'I knew him. He was called "Mad" because he was the reverse. Unemotional—cold, calculating, ruthless bastard.'

'With those friends in high places.'

'Right. He had money, too. The gaol break must have cost him a bit. Yeah, he could've gone for plastic surgery.' Frank touched the side of his face. 'He had a knife scar here. Very distinctive. And he could've set Heysen up for a fall to get him out of circulation and warn him to keep his mouth shut.'

I thought that over and didn't like it. 'I can't see it, Frank. Why wouldn't Heysen use what he knew about Sawtell as a bargaining chip to get out of the charge against him?'

Frank shrugged. 'I don't know, but the thing just has a whiff of Sawtell about it. Devious was his middle name, if it wasn't vicious. Trouble was, he had charm and a sense of humour and people liked him. Especially women.'

'What about the scar?'

'Distinctive, but didn't disfigure him. Badge of honour. Didn't put the women off. Let's have a look at these others. James Ashley Whitmont, that'd be Jimmy White if my memory serves. Rapist, skipped bail and vanished. Had money but no brains. Not his sort of thing. Alexander Cart-wright. I remember him vaguely. Whistleblower, I think. He went into the witness protection program. Hard work to find him. Anyway, he was old, probably dead now.'

'How old was Sawtell?'

'Forties.'

'So very likely still alive.'

'Yeah, he was a fitness freak. Didn't smoke, exercised. He'd been a good athlete—in the pentathlon at the Rome Olympics, just missed a bronze. But he could be anywhere, not likely to be hanging around Sydney.'

'What would he be doing then?'

'Anybody's guess. Something perfectly legitimate some-where or highly illegal and profitable somewhere else. Or both.'

'That resourceful?'

'Easily, but it hardly matters, Cliff. He's long gone. Probably not in Australia. One of the reasons to change your appearance in a case like his would be to get a passport.'

'I don't agree. Rex Wain was shit scared, as if what he knew could still hurt him. If all this speculation about him's on the money, it could mean Sawtell's still around.'

Frank shrugged, surprising me.

'What does that mean, mate?'

'You could give that to Catherine as a strong suspicion. Might satisfy her.' Frank leaned back in his chair and stretched. 'I have to admit my thinking was all screwed up when Catherine contacted me. Hilde was worried sick about Peter and I didn't know what her mood was going to be from one day to the next. I'm not proud of it, but when Catherine approached me it seemed like . . . something to do, some kind of escape.'

'But not now?'

'No, not now.'

'I hate loose ends, Frank.'

'So do I, but now they don't seem to matter too much—some of them.'

'Meaning?'

'Let me get you another drink. Who's driving?'

'We tossed. Lily lost. She's on a limit of three.'

He went away and came back with a solid scotch with a fair bit of ice. Same for him. Frank had turned his chair around from his desk and I was sitting in the rocker where their cat Bluey, which always hid when guests arrived, usually sat while Frank was working. Frank had small photos of Hilde and Peter on his desk. Space for more.

I sipped the drink. 'Frank? It'd still be a feather in your cap, finding Sawtell.'

'I don't wear the cap anymore and don't need feathers. Come to that, it'd do you more good. I imagine the reward that was up for him's still available. But I want to turn our attention to William Heysen. Let's forget about the old farts. See if something can be salvaged from all this for the young people.'

part two

14

A couple of days later I went to see Catherine Heysen and told her the results of my investigation.

'It's just possible an aggrieved client for illicit plastic surgery arranged to frame your husband, but the only credible candidate is either dead, overseas or totally hidden.'

She was her usual super-composed self. 'I see.'

'Even if that was true, your husband doesn't emerge as an innocent victim and your son's not likely to change his evaluation of him or himself on that account.'

'What if he learned that his father was actually a senior and highly respected policeman?'

'That's another matter. Have you decided whether to go ahead with the DNA test?'

'No.'

'May I ask why not?'

'I don't choose to tell you.'

There was no coffee this time and an even cooler atmosphere. I got up out of my chair. 'Your privilege. That's all I have to say.'

The composure shattered then like a fragile glass ornament dashed to the floor. She buried her face in her hands and sobs racked her body. I stood there, feeling useless. She wasn't the kind of woman you patted on the shoulder and said, 'There, there,' to. When she lifted her head, the carefully arranged hair was a mess and the perfect makeup was smeared and clown-like. Years of keeping up a façade had taken a toll and when the façade collapsed, it collapsed completely. She looked every day of her age, and tired.

Through her sobs she said something in Italian. Then she collected herself and I assume she translated: 'I want my son, I need him.'

'Yes,' I said. 'I can see that you do.'

'I've been a vain and foolish woman, Mr Hardy. I've done nothing useful with the advantages I've had. If I could just save my boy from the awful life he is in, that would be something.'

'Is he Frank Parker's son?'

She moved her hands around her head to smooth her hair and dry her tears. 'I don't know. Does it matter?'

'It doesn't matter to Frank, as you know. Might matter a bit to me.'

She said again: 'I don't know. Will you try to find him for me?'

It wasn't the time to tell her the little I'd teased out about William Heysen so far, but I liked her more at that moment than previously. Her distress was genuine and I'm a sucker for it. But not a soft touch. It'd be a paying job and I could count on Frank's help. I told her I'd try to find him, no matter whose son he was. I said I'd mail her a contract form.

I got the usual stuff together and opened a file with a recent photograph, the names of friends, contacts at SBS—his last place of work—car registration, details of credit cards he used and as close a physical description as his mother could provide. It didn't go much beyond 'tall, slim and handsome with dark hair'. She guessed his height at about six feet and his weight at eleven stone, call it 180 plus centimetres and 70 plus kilos. According to her, he had all his own teeth and no scars. He didn't wear glasses and he'd scarcely ever been ill in his life. He was clean-shaven and short-haired when she last saw him, which didn't mean he was now. She knew of no girlfriends in recent times. I didn't ask about boyfriends.

I spent a couple of days tracking down the friends and former flatmates and workmates. Some I found and some I didn't, but none had seen William Heysen for months. When I questioned them about his character, they all agreed that he was very bright and very unusual. A girl who'd had a brief affair with him said, 'I never knew whether he cared about me or not and in the end it didn't matter because he just stopped seeing me. No explanation, no reason. It was as if I'd never existed. Weird.'

I pressed her, asking about William's personal habits—drink and drugs and the like. She shook her head.

'Didn't drink much, but I remember this one time when I'd taken an eccy and he really sounded off on me. Told me how dangerous they were and how contaminated. He bloody lectured me about how they made them in Indonesia and how everybody got ripped off along the way. Sounded like he knew a bit about it.'

That was worrying. I've never had much to do with the drug community, and the few users I knew—a doctor who'd injected heroin for thirty years without ill effect, an ex-boxer who dealt with the boredom of retirement through the judicious use of cocaine, and a musician who took just about everything for a period, stopped cold turkey for a while to allow himself to recover, and then plunged back in—were of no help. The musician's ecstasy supplier was a biker who only dealt in local stuff because the higher quality imported product was too expensive.

I thumbed through my address book and found the number for Jon Van Hart who, last I heard, worked as a consultant for the drug squad. During my period of suspension, for something to do, I went to as many improving lectures and seminars around town as I could. Van Hart had given a lecture on the manufacture of speed and ecstasy and we'd exchanged a few words and our cards afterwards.

'I remember you,' he said when I got through to his mobile. 'How's it going?'

'Well, I'm back on the job. Looking for a bit of info on ecstasy. I know bugger-all about it or about drugs in general, apart from alcohol, caffeine, aspirin, paracetamol, codeine, pseudo-ephedrine . . .'

He laughed. 'I'll help if I can.'

Stretching my information to the limit, I said, 'I'm hearing noises about someone I'm interested in importing the stuff from South-East Asia.'

'Indonesia?'

'Yes.'

'It's happening all right. There's been some interceptions and the police make a big noise about it, but I know and they know that the ratio of found to undetected is up around one to ten, maybe more.'

'How does it work?'

'I take it you don't want the chemical details?'

'No, the organisational.'

He told me that the stuff came in branded as legitimate pharmaceuticals with all the appropriate documentation, except that it was forged. The traffic relied on a certain level of official corruption at both ends and constant liaison between suppliers, shippers and distributors.

'Lots of comings and goings on entirely legal tourist visas. Tell me about the guy you're interested in.'

'He's young, very bright, studied chemistry, speaks Indonesian and a few other languages.'

'Perfect.'

'Where would I find him?'

'You wouldn't,' Van Hart said.

'Where would I look?'

'In transit.'

I was out of my depth and phoned Frank with the news. He got busy tapping his sources—serving and ex-cops, federal policemen and people in Customs. We met for a drink in a pub in Darlinghurst near the police HQ to compare notes. I'd tried to give the balance of Frank's money back to him but he'd refused to take it. Catherine Heysen had signed and returned the contract and given me a solid retainer so I was on a good earner, which only made it worse that I'd come up empty.

'Me, too,' Frank said. 'Absolutely bugger-all. Some people agree there's a supply coming in from South-East Asia pretty much the way Jon Van Hart laid it out for you. But Customs are in denial, and the intelligence types who used to take an interest are so devoted to finding non-existent terrorists that they've got no time for anything else.'

'D'you reckon the asking around will have got through to William? Ripple effect, sort of?'

'Hard to say. Possibly.'

'I can't think of any way to flush him out,' I said. 'Can't see myself posing as an ecstasy buyer with a preference for the Indonesian variety. Couldn't stand the dance party music, for one thing. Anything happening about the DNA test?'

'I've provided the sample. Takes a while.'

'She says she doesn't know who the father is.'

Frank raised his drink as a toast to nothing in particular. 'That makes quite a few of us.'

The news came through a day after and I picked it up on the radio at 6 pm:

> A woman was shot in Earlwood this afternoon as she got out of her car to check the malfunction of the electronic gate to her driveway. Mrs Catherine Heysen was wounded in the shoulder by a shot fired by a person sitting in a parked car. Mrs Heysen's neighbour, who has asked not to be named, was drawing up near the attacker's car in his Volvo sedan and witnessed the shooting. He sounded his horn and rammed the car, which drove off at high speed. An ambulance was called and Mrs Heysen was taken to the Royal Prince Alfred Hospital where she has been reported to be in a satisfactory condition following an operation to remove the bullet.
>
> The police are investigating. They say Mrs Heysen made a short statement before undergoing surgery. She said she could not think why anyone would want to kill

her, and that her neighbour had saved her life. She said
she thanked him from the bottom of her heart and that
she would compensate him for damage to his vehicle.

'That's typical of her,' I said to Lily, who'd heard the
broadcast. 'Do and say the right thing however you might
be feeling.'

'Gutsy, I'd say.'

'Yeah, but secretive. This must have something to do
with the investigation of Heysen and Padrone or the search
for William Heysen.'

'Or both.'

'Or both. Do you reckon the media'll dig up the stuff
about Heysen and Bellamy?'

Lily considered. 'Possibly, but a lot of the reporters
around now think of everything pre-9/11 as ancient history.
If she'd been killed maybe, but wounded isn't sexy.'

'A photo of her'd take care of that.'

'Really?'

I nodded. 'But she did her modelling under a different
name so they might not twig. It could bring young Billy to
the surface though, if he cares about her.'

'Come on, she's his mother.'

'I told you, he's a cold fish and she hasn't seen hide nor
hair of him in six months.'

'No one's that cold.'

'I hope you're right. If it's got something to do with the
old Heysen and Bellamy matter, I'm back on the same trail,
or two trails.'

'You'll cope.'

'I dunno. I'm a linear thinker. Two lines of thought tend
to confuse me.'

'Bullshit. I have to go out, Cliff. By the way, I had word to-day that my house's nearly finished. Be out of your hair soon.'

She kissed me as she went. That was Lily. That was Lily and me.

I phoned the hospital and asked when Mrs Heysen could receive visitors.

'Family?'

'Friend.'

'She's under heavy sedation.'

'Have family members been in?'

'Who is speaking, please?'

That meant the cops had asked the hospital to monitor calls. Fair enough. I hung up. I went back to my notebook and the page with the boxes and arrows and squiggles and tried to come up with an explanation of why anyone would want to kill Catherine Heysen. There were two possibilities as I saw it: one, that William Heysen was involved in some deep, big money shit, and that our enquiring about him had prompted someone to put an end to that enquiring at the likely source. The second was that my scouting around about the Heysen and Bellamy matter had opened an old, tender wound, and someone thought killing Catherine Heysen might cauterise it. I tended to favour the second scenario and wasn't happy about it. 'Mad Matt' Sawtell was a possibility, and Frank and I were both possible additional targets.

'Watch your back, Frank,' I said when I phoned him.

He'd thought it through the same way. 'Watch your own,' he said.

'This woman's brought you a fair amount of grief already. You don't need any more.'

'I feel embarrassed about this, Cliff. But there's some hold-up with Peter's marriage and the visas and that. Hilde's dead keen for us to go over there and meet the girl and see Peter.'

'You should.'

'It feels like running away.'

'Bullshit. It focuses things. I can arrange protection for Catherine, and if I attract any flak I reckon I can handle it. Someone who shoots at a woman at close range, misses, and gets scared away by a Volvo doesn't worry me too much.'

'What about Lily?'

'How d'you mean?'

'With a partner you're vulnerable. You know that.'

'Lily's house is nearly ready. She'll be gone in a day or so.'

'How do you feel about that?'

'In view of this, good. Do a Peter Allen, mate.' Tunelessly, I chanted, 'Go to Rio, de Janeiro.'

'Christ, that's enough to make me do it.'

I kept phoning the hospital. Complications had set in and Catherine Heysen needed a second operation. She recovered quickly after that. Her shooting had attracted no more media attention and, almost a week after it, when Lily had moved back to Greenwich and Frank and Hilde had flown to South America, I went to the hospital to see her.

15

She had a private room with a view back towards the university colleges. Not bad. The room was full of more flowers than she could smell and more fruit than she could eat, indicating that members of her family had been frequent visitors. She was sitting propped up when I arrived. Her hair was arranged and her makeup was perfect. She wore a pink bed jacket over a silk nightdress and looked about as good as anyone who'd been shot could look.

She extended her left hand. 'Mr Hardy.'

'How are you feeling, Mrs Heysen?'

'Not bad, thank you. The people here are excellent and I have my own doctor keeping an eye on things of course. Please sit down.'

'I know the police will have asked you, but did you see the man who shot you?'

'No, not at all. I don't even know that it was a man.'

'Why d'you say that?'

She shrugged and a grimace of pain crossed her face. 'I must not do that. I don't know—there are terrible people around these days of both sexes.'

'It sounds as if you had some . . . intuition about it.'

'Perhaps. But if I did at the time, it has dissipated now after the operation and the drugs.'

'Can you write? I mean, it's your right shoulder, isn't it?'

'Yes. I wonder. I haven't tried. Why?'

I took one of my cards from my wallet. 'I'd like to talk to the neighbour who helped you. Apparently he wants to stay anonymous. I thought if you okayed it he might talk to me.'

'Mr Lowenstein at number twelve. Yes, I think he might.'

'Do you know him well?'

'I don't know anyone well, Mr Hardy. I obviously didn't know my own husband well. Or my son. If you have a pen I'll write something for Mr Lowenstein, if I can manage.'

I gave her a ballpoint and she found she had full mobility from the elbow down. She wrote on the back of the card and signed it. I thanked her.

'What's this all about, Mr Hardy?'

'As I told you at our last meeting, perhaps you were right all along and someone framed your husband. Frank and I probing into it might have upset that person, who might think you ordered the investigation.'

'Which I did, in a way. But . . .'

'There's no statute of limitation on murder, or on conspiracy to murder, I think. Not much point in finding your son if you're not around to say hello to him.'

'You think this person might try again?'

'It's difficult to say. Do you know what calibre the bullet was?'

'No, but it didn't do a great amount of damage apparently.'

'What was the range?'

She almost shrugged again, but stopped in time. 'Oh, not far, ten metres?'

'Small calibre at that range sounds like a professional. If you persist . . .'

'But I'm not persisting, as you put it. You're looking for William and that's all.'

'This hypothetical person probably doesn't know that.'

She was a perceptive woman. 'There's something you're not telling me.'

'You're right. The news doesn't get any better, Mrs Heysen. Frank and I have put out feelers and there's a possibility that William is involved in something criminal and . . . big. So this attempt on your life could be a warning to him.'

'Oh God, this is horrible.'

'I'm concerned for your safety, and William's.'

'Is Frank?'

It wasn't the time to tell her that Frank was on the way to sorting out the personal problems which had been a part of his response to her initially. But his concern for the son was ongoing, so I said yes.

'When I'm released from here I'm going to stay at my parents' place until I'm fully recovered. I have uncles and nephews. I'll be safe. Then I'm going to sell the Earlwood place and get a flat with state of the art security.'

'That's good,' I said. 'You have my numbers. Please let me know where you are and I'll keep you in touch with our search for your son.'

The session had tired her and she nodded wearily. I went away thinking that she'd originally said she'd hang on to the Earlwood place as a sort of homing device for

William. Did selling it mean she had full confidence in my ability to find him? I didn't think so.

I'd parked semi-legally in a Newtown back street, which was as close as I could get to the hospital. It was a Thursday and busy, with pensions being paid and shops staying open late. I contemplated leaving the car where it was and walking to the office but decided against it. A conscientious parking inspector would certainly book it and I didn't need the expense and the hassle.

The afternoon was cloudy and cool, with the sun low in the sky. The street was shaded by plane trees and three-storey terraces. I hurried to keep warm. I squinted ahead twenty metres to see if there was an infringement notice on the windscreen. There wasn't. I felt for my keys and then I was hurled forward by a blow to the back of my neck. I hit the bonnet of the car and my knees buckled but I fought for balance and twisted around in time to see the baseball bat coming towards me. It seemed as big as a balloon and I knew I was too winded and off balance to avoid it. I just managed to tilt my head away, and the bat caught me a glancing blow above the ear. A shaft of pain shot through me and I went down with my head ringing and my eyes shut tight.

I wasn't unconscious, but I was close to it. I sensed rather than saw a shape loom over me and I felt the bat press down hard at the top of my spine as if the attacker was setting up for the fatal whack.

'Hey, hey you!'

The voice seemed to come from miles away but I could hear heavy running feet. The pressure lifted and I sucked in air. The next thing I heard was the roar of an over-revved engine and the squeal of burning rubber. The smell washed back over me and I vomited into the gutter.

The ringing in my ears dropped to an intermittent hum and stopped. I was bleeding above the ear and my hair was damp and matted. I'd split my lip on the gutter and blood and vomit had dripped down my chin and onto my shirt. I spluttered to get the bits of leaf and dirt and sick out of my mouth. My neck ached and my upper back throbbed as I moved. My thick hair had taken some of the force out of the knock to the head. I felt in my mouth with my tongue. No loose teeth. Could have been worse.

I almost flinched as another shape appeared above me.

'You all right, mate?'

He was a giant, 195 centimetres plus, dressed in running gear. Shoulders like railway sleepers, thighs like tree trunks.

'Shit, he could've killed you.' He pulled a mobile phone, looking like a matchbox in his huge paw, from his shorts. 'Want me to call the cops?'

'No. It's a . . . private matter. I'll settle it. But thanks, you scared him off. Did you see what happened?'

'Yeah, sort of. I was jogging along here and I saw you coming, 'bout fifty metres off. You see there?'

He jerked his thumb over his shoulder. 'That's a narrow little lane runs between these two terraces. I keep an eye open because kids come out on bikes and skateboards and that. I reckon he must've been in there because all of a sudden he's up and bashing you. You're lucky he didn't kill you.'

The head wound had stopped bleeding. I sucked blood from my lip and spat into the gutter, careful to miss him. 'I dunno. Maybe not, but thanks again.'

'Jeez.' He retreated a step. 'What kind of game are you in?'

I reached into my jacket, got my wallet and showed him the PEA licence. It impresses people sometimes. It did him.

'Can you describe the man?' I asked.

'Not really. It was all so quick, like. Fair-sized bloke. Fattish. That's all I can say. I can tell you about his car though.'

'That could help.'

'Red Commodore with a bloody great ding in the back. He was parked just down there. Ran to it when I yelled, got in and went like hell. Nearly lost control on the corner there. You can still smell the rubber.'

'Yeah, the smell made me chuck. Well—'

'Now I come to think of it, he was in a grey suit. That struck me as funny, but I didn't remember first off. I'm sorry I didn't get the number.'

'I'd be worried about you if you had. What game d'you play, as if I need to ask?'

'The game they play in heaven, mate.'

I reached out and up and we shook hands. 'Thanks for the help. Take care of yourself.'

He jogged on the spot a few times and gave a short laugh. 'I reckon it's you who should be doing that, mate.'

I drove home with difficulty. My neck was stiff and I was still sucking blood from my lip. I was glad Lily wasn't there to see me in that state. Not that it would have worried her too much. Her father had been a professional boxer and her brother still was—a good one. She'd seen plenty of split skin and blood.

I hauled myself inside, shucked off the blood- and vomit-stained clothes and stood under the shower for fifteen minutes. I parted the hair around the head gash and decided it didn't need stitching. A caustic stick stopped the lip bleeding and the hot spray had eased the aches in my back. Nothing eased the anger and humiliation. My attacker must have been trailing me and I hadn't noticed. And I hadn't registered the narrow lane right by the car. Getting careless, even though I'd had it in mind that I could be a target.

As therapy, I tried a solid scotch and ice, which seemed to work well enough to give it a second try. The head began to throb again and I took some Panadeine Forte. It kept hurting and I took some more and another drink. The combination closed me down. I went up the stairs with a buzz that was more pleasurable than painful. I fell into bed thinking that I'd like to meet up again with the guy with the baseball bat. Preferably, with him minus the bat, and me with one of my own.

I don't know why it is, and I've never asked anyone else if it's true of them—I suspect it might be—that the lyrics of Bob Dylan songs often run through my head. That day I'd been doing the bit about St Augustine being as alive as you or me, and it triggered a dream in my drugged state. I dreamed my ex-wife Cyn, who'd died of cancer a few years back, and a girlfriend of more recent time, Glen Withers, who was shot dead, were both still alive. I was torn between them, guilty as hell as I lied to first one and then the other. It was one of those impossible to resolve situations that, in the dream, just gets worse and worse.

I woke up sweating although I only had a light cover on the bed. As the dream faded I was aware of feeling sad that both women were dead and relieved that I didn't have to deal with the dream problem. I got up, had a piss, drank some water, considered more pills but decided against them. There was a chance they'd plunge me into another Dylan dream and with Dylan you could go to some pretty dark places, like the tombstone blues. I've stood by enough tombstones to provoke nightmares.

Stasiland was by the bed but it wasn't likely to improve my mood. I turned on the radio and listened to 'Australia Talks Back' on low volume until the voices lulled me to sleep. Speculation about the likely retirement date of John Howard wasn't going to keep me awake for long.

16

I slept late and didn't feel too bad when I got up. It wasn't like those times when I couldn't get out of bed after a belting. I wouldn't be going to the gym for a bit, but I was well able to do the things I had to do. Both wounds had scabbed but only one was visible. My bottom lip was puffed like a collagen injection had gone wrong. Eating was going to be tricky, but as I try not to eat until evening I didn't have to worry about that for a while. Hot coffee was also tricky but essential and I drank most of a pot using the side of my mouth. Anyone watching me would have thought I'd had a stroke. I took a few more pre-emptive painkillers. I was still troubled by the dream around the edge of my consciousness, but none of Bob's lyrics were buzzing in my brain so far.

I drove to Earlwood and pulled up outside number twelve. Like the Heysen house, and the one in between them, it had survived the invasion of the developers. The other two didn't have the same grandeur as the Heysen house, but they were solid California bungalows set on blocks almost as big. The three houses had a defiant look.

At a guess, the native garden mostly took care of itself,

and there were big areas of gravel rather than grass. Way to go. Mr Lowenstein didn't have automated gates to his driveway, just the ordinary kind. They were closed and I could see a white Volvo stationed halfway up the drive.

I went through the gate in the middle of the fence and up a path to the tiled verandah. Cane furniture with cushions. Good sitting area. The solid door featured a stained glass panel but was covered with a heavy security screen. A buzzer was located off to one side of the screen. I buzzed.

The man who answered was elderly, white-haired but bearing up well. He stood confidently behind his screen door, holding the heavy door like a man not expecting trouble but prepared to cope with it by slamming the solid wood.

'Can I help you?' he said.

I held up my licence and the card on which Mrs Heysen had written in a copperplate hand: 'Mr Lowenstein, my deepest thanks for your brave intervention. I would be most grateful if you would talk to Mr Hardy who is working for me. Sincerest thanks.' Her signature, Catherine Heysen, was fluent and legible.

'I saw Mrs Heysen in the hospital yesterday,' I said. 'She assured me she hadn't given your name to anyone but the police and me, and won't in the future. She respects your wish to remain anonymous. I'm trying to find out why she was shot at and—'

Lowenstein waved his hand to silence me. He'd lifted the spectacles suspended around his neck up to operational to study the documents. Apparently satisfied, he nodded, dropped the glasses back to their original position, and unlatched the screen door. 'Papers and notes can be forged,' he said, 'but I've seen you arrive at Mrs Heysen's house before, so I'm inclined to trust you. Please come in. How is the poor woman?'

I went into a dim hallway with a carpet runner. The walls were lined with paintings or framed photographs, I couldn't tell which. Lowenstein carefully relatched the screen door and let the other door swing closed. He moved well, considering his age, which I'd have put at closer to eighty than seventy. He glided past me, heading for some light at the end of the passage.

'She's recovering,' I said. 'Very grateful to you.'

'It was nothing, but I certainly don't want those television reporters who can't pronounce words correctly or speak a grammatical sentence swarming around.'

I'd recently heard an ABC newsreader pronounce the French name Georges as 'Jorgez', so I knew what he meant.

'That won't happen,' I said.

'Good.'

He opened a door leading to a kitchen stocked with scrubbed pine furniture and fittings and with light flooding in through large windows.

'I was having coffee. Would you like some? I must say you look a bit the worse for wear. Interesting how we seem unable to talk without drinking something. Have you noticed that?'

'I have. Yes, thank you.'

He poured the coffee and we sat at the table with the milk and sugar within reach. I took both; my system would be jumping with this much caffeine in me and I needed to dilute it and give the metabolism something to work on.

'Now, what do you want to ask?'

'I know the police will have put this to you already, but did you get a good look at the man who shot Mrs Heysen?'

'No.'

'Did you get an impression of size?'

'Good question. Put that way, yes. It was a biggish car and I could see head and shoulders well up, so I'd say—a big person, larger than average.'

'What kind of car was it?'

He smiled. 'There you have me. I can't identify cars at all, apart from Volvos and VW Beetles. Sorry. This was a large red sedan.'

'That helps,' I said. 'Would you mind telling me how long you've lived here, Mr Lowenstein?'

'Let me see. I bought it when I got my chair. That must be nearly forty years ago. I've been retired for fifteen years.'

'I'm sorry, I should be calling you Professor. What was your field?'

'Psychology. I had a chair at Sydney University.'

'So you knew Dr Heysen and everything that happened back then?'

'Yes and no. Are you having difficulty drinking with that damaged lip?'

'A little, but I'll manage. It's good coffee. What d'you mean by yes and no?'

'I took a sabbatical just before the matter broke, and then I took leave and worked in America for three years. I heard about it when I came back, but it had all more or less blown over by then. The Heysen house was rented. Mrs Heysen didn't return for some years after that.'

'What were your impressions of Heysen?'

'A detestable man—arrogant, conceited and an anti-Semite.'

'What makes you say that?'

'One can tell, Mr Hardy. One can tell.'

'So you can tell that I'm not?'

'Yes.'

'Good. What about the boy, William?'

'I'm tempted to trot out the clinical cliches—only child, precocious, a mother's boy without a valid male role model. All true, I think, to a greater or lesser degree. He was nothing like his father in manner, nothing at all. He'd sky a ball over the fence now and then and come and ask for it. Very polite.'

'You aren't next door and they're wide blocks.'

'He told me he had his mother throw tennis balls to him in their yard for him to practise his defensive strokes. It's hard to imagine such an elegant creature doing that, but I suppose she did. Sometimes he caught one on the rise in the meat of the bat. I played grade cricket myself when I was young. I knew what he meant.'

I remembered playing backyard cricket in Maroubra with my mates. Over the fence was out for six. I don't think any of us ever put it over more than one fence, let alone two. But then, we were more interested in surfing.

'A big hit,' I said.

'He was an athletic young man. Mother-fixated, I should say, with all that that implies.'

'You mean that he loved and hated her at the same time?'

'Exactly. My wife thought very highly of him. She was Italian and she said he spoke the language fluently and well. The only child we had died as an infant and she liked to take young people under her wing. She thought William had an exceptional linguistic gift.'

It was one of those moments when you respect a person's emotional space and I was glad I had the coffee cup to fiddle with. The pause was brief.

'She's been dead for ten years,' he said. 'I should sell this place. I've had offers enough, God knows, but I can't seem to get around to it. Something about the sums they mention and the way they talk puts me off. And I must confess I take an interest in the rehabilitation of the river, slow as it is. It's never been clean in my time, but I believe it once was, with sandy banks. People swam and fished in it, I'm told.'

'Hard to believe,' I said.

'Yes. Would you mind telling me what you're actually doing for Mrs Heysen?'

'Several things.'

'Now you're being secretive. I thought frankness was your style.'

'You're right, Professor. As I said, I'm concerned about the attempt on Mrs Heysen's life and I don't know its source.' I touched my scabby lip. 'The shooting was a professional job gone wrong, and I've had a narrow miss as well. Apart from that, I'm trying to locate William Heysen. His mother hasn't had any contact with him for some months and there's a strong possibility he's in serious trouble.'

'I'm sorry to hear that. Are you saying he's . . . missing?'

'Effectively, yes. I've contacted people he lived with and worked with and none of them have—'

'Seen him, you're about to say. But I have. He was here, at the house. Just a few days ago.'

17

I almost dropped the coffee cup. 'You saw him? When was this?'

Professor of Psychology or not, he looked as pleased by my reaction to his statement as anyone would have been. 'Happily, I'm not afflicted by short-term memory loss like so many people my age. This was three days ago.'

'What happened?'

'I was sitting on the front verandah, reading. It catches the afternoon sun. I saw a car pull up outside the Heysen house. Cars, again. All I can say is that it wasn't the car William used to drive when he lived here. This was a big car, a four-wheel drive model—' he waved his hands to illustrate the style—'and black. As I say, not his old car, but definitely him.'

'Did you speak to him?'

'No, no. I'm sure he didn't even see me. I suppose I assumed he'd been to see his mother and was fetching something from the house for her. I didn't know anything about him being missing. He went in.'

'How long did he stay?'

'I'm afraid I don't know. I went inside to make some

notes on what I'd been reading. I still do some research and writing, you see. I didn't go to the front again at all that day. The car had gone by the next day but he could have been there five minutes or five hours.'

'How did he look? Confident? Furtive?'

'Really, Mr Hardy, you ask the most extraordinary questions. I only glimpsed the boy for a few seconds.'

'Your impression?'

He thought. I suppose psychologists think a lot and don't need any props to do it. His cup stayed on the table and he didn't scratch himself or tent his fingers. He just sat. 'Preoccupied,' he said at last. 'As you'd expect.'

I nodded. Preoccupied perhaps, but not about his mother, who he hadn't contacted. It was unlikely that he hadn't heard about the shooting. I thanked him for giving me his time.

He smiled. 'The odd thing about my situation is that in one way I have all the time in the world and in another, who knows? Maybe not much.'

'I think you're good for a few years yet.'

We moved back into the passage. 'I hope so. I still enjoy life. I'm glad to have met you, Mr Hardy. I haven't encountered many—what should I say, men of action?—in my life. You'd make an interesting case study.'

'I don't think so.'

'Oh, yes. You're drawn to intrigue and violence like a moth to a flame.'

I drove to the office mulling over what Professor Lowenstein had said, both about my character and his sighting of William Heysen. Intrigue went with the territory, but was it true that I welcomed violence? Cyn had always said so and she, like the professor, was very smart. I didn't think of myself that way, but I knew I'd been involved in violence for the greater part of my life—from boxing as an adolescent in the police boys' club, through military service and on into my career as a PEA. I decided that it was only partly true. I'd done the things I'd done not primarily because I sought the violence involved, but because I rejected the alternatives—the passive life, the routines. That satisfied me on that score.

I parked, climbed the stairs and went into the office. The building is old and in poor repair. After my little nook had been closed up for a few days the general decay of the place seemed to creep in as a smell. But it's probably just the cockroaches and mice—some dead, some alive—in the wall cavities. I sometimes wondered what the space I rented had been used for in the past. I once found a threepenny bit in the skirting board and a stiff, brittle condom caught in the slats of the venetian blind. Doesn't tell you a lot but gives you ideas.

The sighting of young Heysen, apparently prosperous, had to be a positive. Up to that point, given Rex Wain's 'whisper', there had been a chance he wasn't in the country. But why does a mother-fixated son not visit that mother in hospital? Because he can't? Lowenstein could have mistaken preoccupation for worry. Whatever the reason, it hadn't brought me any closer to finding him.

I made some notes on the conversation with the Prof and couldn't help underlining a phrase—He was nothing like his father . . . The conversation had left me with questions to add to the list I already had: why had William Heysen gone to the house? What, if anything, had he taken, or left? Would Catherine Heysen allow me to search the house? Where was William living? How many black 4WDs are there in Sydney? Not all of the questions I jot down at these moments are sensible.

The coffee and paracetamol buzz was fading and my abused back was aching. A big man in a red Commodore. I was looking for bright and dull coloured cars in a city full of cars. Needles in a very big haystack. As I looked at my notes and doodles, I came close to being sure of one thing, more a matter of intuition than logic: the attacks on Catherine Heysen and me had to do with the old Heysen–Bellamy matter, not Billy boy.

The phone rang.

'Hardy.'

'This is William Heysen.'

I was surprised, but not as surprised as I would have been a few hours earlier.

'Oh, yeah? The William Heysen who drives a black 4WD and doesn't visit his mother in hospital when she's been shot?'

'Do you want to talk, or just make smartarse remarks?'

'You talk, I'll listen.'

'I understand you've been looking for me.'

'Right, on behalf of your mother.'

'Yes, but before she was shot.'

'True.'

'Why?'

'It's a long story. It goes back to Dr Gregory Heysen.'

'My father, the murder conspirator.'

'I have to tell you there's some doubt about that.'

'What? That he wasn't guilty?'

'Possibly. I think we should meet. There are . . . things to discuss.'

'Such as?'

I had to think about that. The whole matter of his paternity was hanging fire and could go either way. But I had him on the hook and didn't want to lose him. I couldn't think of a better bait.

'The identity of your father.'

'What do you mean?'

'We need to talk. Where are you, William?'

'Patronise me, and you'll never hear from me again.'

Nasty. Maybe he was the doctor's son.

'I'm sorry.'

'Is your enquiry in any way to do with the police?'

That was a curly one if only he knew it. But I played a straight bat. 'No.'

'All right. We'll talk.'

'Where are you?'

A few seconds elapsed and then the door swung in and a tallish young man stood there, lowering a mobile phone from his ear. 'Right here.'

I couldn't stop myself. 'Who's the smartarse now?' I said.

'Melodramatic, I'll agree.'

He came in and dropped down into the client chair. He was very much as his mother had described him—not quite as tall, slim, dark-haired with an olive tint to his skin, handsome and aware of it. Too aware. He was clean-shaven; his hair was long but neat. He wore loose pants, a T-shirt and a denim jacket, all pricey, all clean. If he was on drugs they hadn't taken any toll on him yet. He sat straight in the chair and looked at me with a confident manner, bordering on cockiness.

'What's this about my paternity?'

'Let's back up a bit,' I said. 'How did you find out about me?'

He didn't want to concede anything but apparently decided to yield a fraction. 'I found your card in the house. I also heard an answering machine message from you that dated back a bit. Plus, a person I know told me you'd contacted her asking questions. Satisfied?'

'That fits. Why haven't you visited your mother? Why drop out of sight?'

He shook his head. 'That's all I'm saying until I hear more from you.'

I wasn't used to fencing with someone so much younger, but there was something steely about him that made it necessary. 'I should really get your mother's permission to tell you this, but when you went off the rails after you found out about your father, she—'

His poise slipped for the first time. 'What? She said that?'

'Yes.'

The composure returned almost immediately, shades of his mother. 'Incredible. Go on.'

This was getting tricky. I didn't want to tell him about Frank and the paternity test and all the rest of it. Not yet, anyway. I swivelled around creakily in my chair that needed oiling and probably more than that. I stared out the window for a moment in the hope of unsettling him. It worked.

'Well?' He was a bit off balance now.

'Look, William, you're the one sneaking around, hiding, making furtive visits, worried about whether I'm tied in with the police. You're obviously in some kind of trouble. I suggest you change your attitude.'

He didn't like it, but he didn't get up and leave. 'I'll tell you this,' he said quietly. 'That woman's a monster. She's so manipulative she doesn't know what she's doing half the time. I didn't go off the rails, as you put it, because I discovered my father was a criminal. I simply experimented with a different lifestyle for a while. I'd played the role of the achieving son for so long I was sick and tired of it. I knew she was living through me, having somehow stalled in her own life. Then I saw a . . . an opportunity and pursued it.'

'Which has put you in danger.'

'Maybe, but I believe I can handle it. There, I've put some cards on the table. Your turn. I'm interested in this paternity business, but it's almost certainly one of her fantasies. If that's the basis of your investigation, you're on a hiding to nothing.'

'It's a bit more than that. There's a strong possibility Dr Heysen was framed and that the person who did it wants no enquiry. I think that's why your mother was shot and why I was attacked.'

'The mouth,' he said. 'And the stiff neck.'

He was smart and observant. 'Exactly. I'm sure you're relieved to learn that your mother being shot wasn't to do with you and your activities.'

'You're on the wrong tack there, Mr Hardy. I never for a minute thought that was a possibility. You've met her. How many enemies do you think she's been capable of making?'

'Whether that's true or not, she's your mother and you don't seem very concerned about her.'

'Oh, I know she's all right.'

'How?'

'I went in there, into the hospital. I'd changed my appearance somewhat. I got close enough to see that she's not in danger and is getting the best of care.'

'No thanks to you.'

'She doesn't need help from me. She's never needed help from anyone. Either that, or she needs so much help she's beyond helping.'

'I think you've worked on that line.'

He let that pass, which probably meant I was right. 'We seem to have reached a stalemate. Are you going to enlighten me about this paternity business or not?'

'You're curious?'

'Who wouldn't be? Most people have a changeling complex at some time or other.'

I had to think what to say. He'd come to me so I suppose I could say I'd found him. Job completed, at least the unstated job of locating him. But he was likely to vanish again and there was nothing to prove I'd seen him. But there was still the original question and its probable aftermath—the attacks on Catherine Heysen and myself. Would she want to employ me on that? Or was I still on it on Frank's behalf? Confusing.

'I think your mother should tell you about it,' I said.

'No chance. I don't care if I never see her again.'

'She's planning to sell the house.'

He shrugged. 'It's hers to sell.'

'You have an interest.'

'Not interested.'

'Meaning you've got all the money you're ever going to need?'

'I wouldn't say that, but . . .'

I was at the end of my patience with him. 'You're full of shit, William. You've got an opportunity, you say. Okay, you're going to make big bucks. But you haven't made them yet and you've got a few problems. Just possibly, I could help you there, get you out from under.'

I could almost see the brain wheels turning. I still didn't like him, but there was no denying his smarts. No nervous gestures from him though; he was still in control as he weighed the odds. 'Out from under,' he said. 'Strange expression. I don't have any problems. What makes you think I do?'

'I've been told you're smuggling drugs in from Indonesia.'

He threw back his head and the laugh that came from him was genuine and full-hearted, perhaps with a touch of relief in it. 'Me? Smuggling drugs? That's the dumbest thing I've ever heard. Every link in that chain is compromised. More money changes hands for information and corruption than ever gets made by anyone involved. It's a high risk business, too high.'

'Sounds as though you've considered it.'

'Oh yes.'

'I've got that from two sources.'

'Well, I might've given some people that impression. Look, if I tell you what I'm on about, or give you an idea of it, will you tell me what I want to know?'

'I guess. If you'll contact your mother, confirm that you've spoken to me and that you're alive and well.'

'Protecting your arse. All right. I don't like it but all right.'

'Unship your mobile and do it now.'

He didn't like that, but he'd painted himself into a corner. He rang the hospital and asked to be put through to the ward. 'Mother?' he said.

I came around the desk and heard Catherine Heysen's distinctive voice, perhaps less confident than it had been previously. 'William, is that you?'

'Yes, Mother. I'm talking to your private detective with

the split lip and the aching back—Mr Hardy, in his Newtown office. Here he is.'

He was full of tricks. I took the phone, said a few words and then busied myself making coffee. The conversation obviously didn't go well for either of them, but it met my stipulation. He closed off the call as the coffee maker began its geriatric process.

'Satisfied?' he said.

'Yeah. So what's your game?'

He put the tiny phone back in his jacket pocket and I wondered if he'd used it to take a photograph or record the conversation or do any of the hundred and one things they're capable of doing these days. From his smug self-satisfied look it seemed possible, but he was still the one who had had to ante up first.

'I suppose you could say I'm into immigration facilitation.'

18

'People-smuggling,' I said.

He shook his head. 'That reeks of leaky boats and sleazy types fleecing ignorant peasants. I deal at the top end of the market.'

Add conceit to the list of his unpleasant characteristics. 'Which means?'

'Mr Hardy, I speak Arabic, Indonesian, Urdu, Tamil and a few other languages. When I apply myself, I can pick up a working knowledge of a language in a matter of weeks. As a consequence, I have contacts in many places—consulates, embassies. Anyone who arrives in this country under my auspices arrives in comfort with convincing documentation.' He laughed and did a very fair imitation of the bleating voice of John Howard. 'I will decide who comes to this country.'

'For a price.'

'Naturally, but with full value for money.'

'I wouldn't say I was totally out of sympathy with that, but it's still an illegal activity and the penalties are heavy.'

'There won't be any penalties. Now, suppose you enlighten me about my paternity.' His good-looking face was suddenly less attractive wearing a sneer. 'I'll tell you one thing—it wasn't a virgin birth. She . . . never mind.'

Referring to my notebook, I told him the story without the names. He listened closely and I had the feeling that he was committing every detail to memory. The coffee machine went quiet and I took two polystyrene cups from the desk drawer and held one up.

'No,' he said. 'So he was crooked anyway, whether or not he set up his partner's death.'

I'd expected him to comment on his mother's doubt about his paternity and I said so. I poured the coffee and sipped it. Bitter as usual—perhaps more bitter than usual.

He waved a hand dismissively. 'Couldn't care less. Almost certainly a fantasy of hers to draw this bloke into her web. She's done similar things before. Anyway, the nature or nurture debate doesn't interest me much. If the nature includes a criminal doctor or a policeman it doesn't matter. The nurture was lousy. All pretence on both our parts. I consider that I made myself what I am.'

'That's very arrogant.'

'Depends on your standpoint. I'm more interested in this idea that an aggrieved client from the past could want to shut you both down. That's intriguing. How do you plan to handle it?'

'Not sure why I should tell you, but I will. First, make sure she's safe. I was told to drop it, but I'm going to persist in the hope that it draws the person out.'

'A Judas goat?'

Somehow you don't expect the young, brought up on television and video games, to know about such things, but William Heysen was a surprise package.

'Something like that.'

'Might work, or you might get yourself killed.'

'So might you unless you get out of the business you're in and take yourself off somewhere.'

He stood and stretched. 'When do the results of the paternity test come through? I noticed there was some stuff missing from my room.'

'I don't know. But the man I spoke of is willing to help you whatever the result.'

He flashed a smile. 'Oh, Jesus, he's in love with her, is he?'

'No.'

'Probably is. Wouldn't be the first. She always had a thing for uniforms. Well, that's very big of him and he might come in useful some day. I suppose I can get in touch with him through you?'

'That depends.'

'On what?'

'On whether I decide you're worth helping.'

'Good point.' He pulled his car keys from his pocket and put them on the desk while he adjusted the sit of his pants. 'Don't try to follow me, please. That'd be very annoying.'

He strolled out and I let him go having the last word. If I'd responded he would've just come back with something smart anyway. I checked his DOB in my notes. He was twenty-four. Too old to be called precocious, too young to be called wise except in the American sense—a wiseguy. He might have considered that he'd made himself and downplayed nature and nurture, but he was his mother's son to a tee. The same conceit, arrogance and composure, the same quick grasp of what was going on and how to turn it to advantage.

He wasn't quite as smart as he thought, though. His car keys had a tag with the registration number on it. I'd memorised it and now I wrote it down. I scribbled notes on the encounter, catching some of his expressions—verbal and physical. It was easy to see the schoolboy athlete in him, and easy to believe that he could learn a language at the drop of a hat. For all that, there was something missing in him, some lack. He was cold, but it was more than that. I couldn't put my finger on it and registered the feeling on the page with a large question mark. One thing was for sure, though—I knew I'd be seeing him again.

Somehow, someone had been keeping an eye on me. There were ways to find that someone, strategies. I could walk or drive to certain places; there were people I could contact to watch me being watched and take action. Unless the watcher was super-professional and very experienced these strategies would work and I was prepared to use them when the time came. For the moment I wanted whoever it was to know that I hadn't abandoned the Heysen enquiry. I rang the hospital and arranged to see Catherine Heysen. It was typical of her not to call me after William had been in touch. The employer doesn't run after the employee.

It was no great distance from the office to the hospital and I decided to walk it. Rain was threatening, but I had a hooded slicker and I've never minded walking in the rain in the right protective gear. Besides, the slicker gave me somewhere to put my .38 Smith & Wesson automatic. 'Judas goat' wasn't quite the right expression. The Judas goat is tethered and helpless, and I wasn't going to be either.

I'm getting to like King Street. It's almost never empty
and for a city man like me that's a plus. Too much space and
too much emptiness give me the creeps unless it's the ocean,
and that's never really quiet or empty. I once counted the
eateries between the railway station and Bob Gould's mad
secondhand book emporium. I forget the number but it
was a lot. I was too early as usual and my back was hurting,
so I stopped for an early afternoon drink and some
painkillers at the pub on the corner of Missenden Road.

I wasn't overconfident about being tracked. I had the
pistol after all. I felt exposed. That pub's one where you can
turn in quickly and see what passes by and that's exactly
what I did. No big guys with baseball bats, no dinged red
Commodores. Apart from being cautious, who ever heard
of a private eye turning up for an interview without alcohol
on his breath?

Catherine Heysen was just back from physiotherapy. She
wore a different nightgown and jacket but was her usual
immaculate self. She was sitting in a chair by the bed with
a number of magazines around her. The hand she extended
was almost welcoming.

'So you found him. Well done, Mr Hardy. Please sit
down. Would you care for some fruit?'

'No, thanks. He more or less found me, but he was
responding to the enquiries I made so I'll take the credit.'

'I'm sure you deserve it. Well, where is he living and
what is he doing? Is it very bad?'

I filled her in on my interviews with the professor and
with her son. I told her what he was doing, or attempting
to do, and that I didn't know where he was living. I didn't

tell her that I could probably find him when I needed to. It never hurts to keep something up your sleeve. I also told her that he'd seen her in hospital.

She shook her head. 'No. I don't believe it, even of him.'

'He said he was in some sort of disguise. He satisfied himself that you were recovering and getting good care, and left without letting you see him.'

The pain in her eyes was about the most expressive reaction I'd seen from her. She dropped her head to conceal it. 'Ah,' she said, 'so he told you all sorts of things about our . . . relationship.'

'Mrs Heysen, I've had a version of that from you, one from him, and another from Professor Lowenstein. They don't match, but that's not my concern.'

All the noblesse oblige was suddenly back. 'And what is?'

'Whether you want me to find out why the murder of Bellamy and the conviction of your husband has led to the threat to you . . . and to me. To be fair, I have to tell you that your son said that finding out about Dr Heysen's conviction had nothing to do with his life choices. But he is interested.'

'You told him about Frank?'

'Not by name. We fenced, exchanging information, and I had to tell him about your belief that he isn't your husband's son. He said he couldn't care less about that.'

'Did you believe him?'

I shrugged. 'Hard to tell. He's very bright and . . . supple.'

'The DNA test result should be through any day now. It'll go to both Frank and me. What's your guess, Mr Hardy?'

'Wouldn't care to make one. I'd say in the important ways, he's like you.'

She smiled at that and, although it produced lines on her face, it emphasised that she would retain a kind of beauty all her life. 'I'm not sure you mean that as a compliment. I don't want to look over my shoulder for the rest of my days. Yes, Mr Hardy, I want you to pursue it. Find out who shot me and attacked you and why. Will you need more money?'

'Not yet. Maybe later.'

'As I said, I have enough. When I sell the house, more than enough. Did you tell him about that? Of course you did, he would have drawn it out. What did he say?'

'He was indifferent.'

'Yes, he would be. He spent as little time there as he could. How dangerous is this business he's in?'

'Very, I'd say, but he was confident he could deal with it in every way. I'd say he's too confident to be fully in touch with reality.'

'Quite the psychologist, aren't you?' she said, sounding just like her son—and with her head tilted and her hair drawn back, she almost looked like him despite the gender and physiological differences. 'You don't like him and you don't like me, but you can't afford to choose who you work for, can you?'

'I can, up to a point. In any case—'

'In any case you're involved in this more in Frank's interest than mine.'

I shifted uneasily in the hard chair and decided to stand. I'd had enough of the hospital smell and of her. 'No, Mrs Heysen, Prof Lowenstein said I was drawn to intrigue and violence like a moth to a flame. Your case has got the lot.'

The beautifying smile spread around her face again.

'You're quite supple yourself, Mr Hardy. I wonder how many lies William told you about me.'

'I wonder, too.'

That actually drew a laugh. She took a moment to collect her thoughts and tidying the magazines seemed to help her. I noticed her wince as she stretched her right arm further than she'd intended. I've had shoulder injuries; they're a bastard to endure, and slow to come right.

When the magazines were lined up to her satisfaction, she leaned back in the chair and let out a long sigh. 'I'll be out of here in a few days. As I told you, I'll be safe in the bosom of my family.'

I nodded. Said nothing, not wanting to push it. Catherine Heysen was not to be pushed.

'Yes,' she said, 'I have every confidence in you. Find out, if you can, what the hell is going on.'

That was uncharacteristic and revived my doubts about her. It often seemed that she was like an actor, working from her own script, but it was the go-ahead I needed.

They picked me up on the hospital steps. They had the bulk. The suits, the shoes. They showed me their warrant cards—Detective Sergeant Wilson Carr and Detective Constable Joseph Lombardi.

'We need to talk to you, Mr Hardy,' Carr said.

'At your disposal. What say we go to the pub across the way and you can shout.'

Neither smiled. Carr said, 'You're coming with us to Surry Hills to answer a few questions.'

You don't argue with them but you don't show fear if

you can help it. 'My lucky day,' I said. 'I walked here so I won't get a parking ticket.'

They escorted me to a car driven by a uniform. Lombardi got in the back with me and Carr got in the front.

'What would this be about?' I said.

Carr half turned and spoke over his shoulder: 'It'd be about you shutting up until we get there.'

We all preserved silence on the drive. I hadn't had much to do with cops in recent times but they never really change. They've got a tough job and there's a lot about police culture that makes it still tougher. There are rotten apples in many barrels and no one quite knows how many and in what barrels. Frank Parker once said the job was like playing football with the members of the two teams changing every few minutes along with the rules. Confusing.

At the Police Centre I was taken to an interview room and set down to wait. At least it wasn't like the old days when the decor was early fifties and you could imagine the slaps from the telephone books and the smell of Craven A cork tips. The room was carpeted, the chairs were upholstered and the table was round. Chummy, almost. The worst that could be said about it was that the air conditioning was a touch low and I was a little overdressed for the temperature.

Carr and Lombardi came in and the junior man got the recording equipment up and running but didn't activate it. They'd obviously been in discussion with someone higher up and didn't seem quite so confident.

'This is just an informal talk,' Carr said.

'Okay. Mind if I invite my solicitor along?'

'That won't be necessary. A few questions, the right answers, a little cooperation, and you're on your way.'

'With a Cabcharge voucher back to Newtown?'

Carr drew in a deep breath. He removed his suit coat and hung it over the back of his chair, giving himself time to get composed. When Lombardi went to do the same Carr stopped him. If this was good guy, bad guy it was hard to interpret. They were uneasy with each other as well as with me.

'Why did you visit Mrs Heysen in hospital?' Carr said.

'She's a family friend.'

'You're determined to piss me off, aren't you, Hardy?'

I shrugged, looked at Lombardi, and very deliberately slipped out of my jacket. 'You've got your job to do and I've got mine.'

'Mrs Heysen's late husband was convicted of conspiracy to commit murder. Now she's been shot. A private detective known to us as a troublemaking arsehole visits her. We want to know why.'

'Did you ask her?'

'She wasn't cooperative. Seems to have a prejudice against the police service.'

I shook my head. 'I can't think why anyone would feel like that.'

'Let me put it this way. A serious crime has been committed and you're withholding information.'

'Let me put it another way,' I said. 'You're suddenly interested enough in this to bring me down here. Why? You show me yours and I might show you mine, if I have anything to show.'

The two exchanged nods. Carr stood and picked up his jacket.

'Okay, Hardy,' he said, 'have it your way. But we've just about had enough of you and your cowboy games. You've done time for conspiracy to pervert the course of justice and destroying evidence. You ought to see the file we have on you.'

'I'd like to.'

'That's exactly what I mean. You love to take the piss, don't you? I'll tell you this—your old mate, former Deputy Commissioner Frank Parker, can't protect you now. We'll be keeping a close eye on you and the reality is that your fucking licence to operate in your crummy profession is hanging by a thread. One false step and you're gone and good riddance.'

I stood and lifted my jacket from the chair. Lombardi stood and we three big men faced off with the tension crackling between us. Again, in the old days it would have been dangerous and I would've expected to get hurt. Not now.

Lombardi went to the door and swung it open so that it crashed back against the wall. A uniformed officer standing there jumped at the noise.

'He'll see you out,' Lombardi said. 'Piss off!'

19

Over the next week and a bit I tried to show that I was still on the case. I went to the hospital without actually seeing Catherine Heysen, but giving that impression. I took a good look at the rear end of every medium-sized red sedan I came across. Anyone watching me would have known what that meant. I went to a Target store and bought a baseball bat, which I left on the front passenger seat of the Falcon. I carried the .38 and I watched my back. Nothing happened.

Frank, back from his flit to Brazil, phoned me at the office. He told me that he and Hilde had taken to Peter's intended, Ramona, straight off. He said the feelings seemed to be mutual and that arrangements to get the pair of them home were proceeding smoothly. I made the right approving noises.

'But that's not what I want to talk to you about,' Frank said. 'The DNA test result's come through. It's positive in that it says there's only one chance in a couple of hundred thousand that the boy's not my son.'

'How's Hilde taking it?'

'She's okay with it. Not enraptured, but . . . interested and a bit more than that. Any luck locating him?'

I told him more or less what I'd told Catherine Heysen, but in starker terms. He listened without interrupting, the way he does.

'We'd better meet,' he said when I'd finished.

'Yeah. She's also hired me to continue the investigation into the Heysen case and the attacks on us.'

There was a pause before he spoke. 'You said us. Has she got to you the way she got to me?'

'No.'

'Good. I told you I'd back you on that—looking for the kid and all the rest of it.'

'I'd rather take her money than yours. You're right, we should meet. Let's make it as public a place as possible.'

'Why?'

'I'll tell you when I see you.'

Centennial Park seemed as good a bet as any other, and we met there mid-morning on a grey day. All the better for there being fewer people about and making it easier to spot anyone suspicious. But there are always walkers, joggers, rollerbladers and cyclists, so the park is never empty.

We met at the Oxford Street gates and strolled in. Straightaway Frank's trained eye spotted that I was carrying my pistol in a shoulder holster under my jacket.

'Why the gun?' he said.

I explained about my Judas goat strategy.

'Thanks a lot,' he said. 'I just love wandering about to be sniped at.'

'I'm going to take steps.'

'Like?'

'The .38 for one, and hiring Hank Bachelor to watch my back. You remember him, the big Yank with the stun gun?'

'He's capable. Who else?'

I mentioned two other PEAs I could call on and Frank nodded approvingly. 'It's going to cost.'

'What d'you reckon her house in Earlwood's worth? She's selling it.'

Frank agreed and I was relieved to see that he'd apparently got over his obsession with Catherine Heysen. I'd told him she was going to stay with her family where there were willing men and he didn't question me further.

'So we're still in a double-barrelled operation here,' Frank said. 'Trying to latch on to whoever's worried about the old business and getting William on the straight and narrow.'

We reached a bench near the pond where Sallie-Anne Huckstepp had been drowned. We sat and looked out over the murky water. If the predictions were right, it'd one day be a home to cane toads. Those thoughts didn't help my mood.

'There's something else, Frank,' I said. I told him about my encounter with the two detectives and my feeling that someone higher up was taking an active interest in matters concerning Catherine Heysen.

'Jesus,' Frank said, touching his nose. 'It never goes away—the stink. I told you something was wrong about the way the Heysen thing played out.'

'Right,' I said. 'But for all that's happened I don't get a sense of having made much progress.'

'Nothing new in that for you, is there, Cliff?'

'No, I guess not. Things take time to come together and sometimes they just don't.'

We went quiet for a while, staring at the water and the grass and the trees as if the answers lay there. They didn't, and a roar of snarled traffic at a distance cut through the quiet of the park.

'Anyway,' I said, 'you've made some progress on life's journey, Grandad.'

'Fuck you,' he said, but he smiled broadly.

Twenty-four hours after meeting Frank I was in the office wondering whether it was time to hunt down William Heysen when I got a call from Hank Bachelor.

'Bingo,' Hank said. 'That's the expression, isn't it? Some guy made several passes of your place. Then he made a sortie out to Lane Cove. I guess that's where the lady's holed up, right?'

'Right.'

'Went by your place again not long ago. Want me to brace him, Cliff?'

'Shit, no. Just keep tabs on him. Tell me he's driving a red Commodore with a dent in the back.'

'You're psychic.'

'That's right. Describe him, will you.'

'He doesn't get out of the car much. I'd say he's about . . .'

'You're breaking up.'

'. . . grey suit . . . porker . . . sonofabitch . . .'

'What? What?'

The line went dead. I swore and sat with scraps of information running through my head. It was half an hour before Hank came back on the line.

'Sorry, Cliff. I lost him. I don't think he spotted me but he turned off and I've gotta admit I lost concentration making the call and when you told me I was breaking up. I backtracked but I couldn't find him.'

'Where are you?'

'Marrickville, around there.'

Things clicked into place. Marrickville. An overweight man in a grey suit. I had a sudden recall of sensations I'd experienced before the baseball bat scrambled my perceptions—a shape, a smell as his foul breath washed over me. Rex Wain!

'It's okay, Hank. I think I know where to find him. Give me a minute to check it out and I'll call you back.'

I grabbed Frank's notes and flicked through them, searching for Wain's address—the place where his phone was about to be cut off, where he hadn't paid the mortgage or probably the rent for months. I found it and called Hank to give him the address.

'Meet me there in ten minutes. Got your tazer?'

He said he did. I got to my car but the ten minutes stretched to twice that as I battled the late afternoon traffic.

The flat was in a small, red brick block close to the railway line and near the border with Dulwich Hill. Hank's 4WD was parked a little past it and on the other side of the street. He knew his business. You don't park immediately outside a place where you expect trouble and you don't let your car door slam. I pulled in a few car lengths further on and gestured for Hank to join me.

He ambled back, all 190 centimetres and 100 kilos of him. I got out and joined him, making sure we couldn't be seen from the flats.

'Car's there, Cliff. Saw it as I went by.'

I nodded. 'This guy's an ex-cop very down on his luck. He took a shot at the woman I told you about and he used a Louisville slugger on me.'

Hank shook his head. 'Didn't think they made 'em anymore. Still, I get your point. Dangerous guy.'

'Could be. Likely to be slow though. He's screwed up twice. Said he didn't have a car. Now he's got one. Means someone's financing him but if he's got money he's drinking. What was his driving like?'

'Lousy. Shit reactions.'

'He's in flat two. Looks like there's only four so two's bound to be ground floor back. If it's okay with you we go in and you knock. He doesn't know you so he'll probably open up. Maybe have the door on a chain. Got anything handy?'

'You want bolt cutters or a tyre iron?'

Hank is nothing if not well equipped. 'Up to you.'

The short street was quiet. No dogs, no skateboarders, no strollers. A train roared past as Hank opened the rear of the 4WD and extracted a solid pair of bolt cutters which he held down by his leg. We crossed the road and went along the cement drive past the line of four skimpy carports to the back of the flats. A faded red Commodore, showing signs of repaired rust and with a deep dint in the back bumper and rear end, was parked a little skewed to one side, cutting down the space for the neighbouring car to get out.

'That'll make him popular,' Hank said.

'His name's Rex Wain, and I don't think he's ever been popular.'

Flat two featured a cheap screw-on number hanging by one screw. Three steps led to the door and parked beside them was a wheelie bin with a cracked top. Beside it a cardboard box overflowed with newspapers and empty stubbies.

Hank knocked and there was no response. We waited, knocked again, same result. I tore off a section of newspaper and tried the handle. The door opened and I stepped inside, straight into the kitchen, with the .38 out and ready.

No need. Rex Wain, in his stained grey suit with the missing buttons, lay face up on the greasy lino floor. He was directly under a bright fluorescent light but the brightness didn't worry him even though his eyes were open. He had a dark hole directly between them and a centimetre or two above. The bench and cupboards behind where he'd been standing were spattered like something from Jackson Pollock, but with blood and pink and grey tissue instead of paint.

20

It was the second time I'd walked Hank Bachelor into a murder scene.

'How do we play it?' he said.

I backed up and ushered him with me. 'We walk away softly,' I said, 'unless you want to spend the next three days with cops in your face.'

'No thanks.'

The other flats were quiet and the street showed no activity. We went back to our cars and drove off with me leading. A few blocks away I stopped and Hank pulled in behind me. He got out and came up to the Falcon, looking casual but probably not feeling it. He got in behind me.

'Wish I smoked,' he said.

'No you don't. What happens is this: I'll call it in anonymously from a payphone. You were never here.'

'What about you? What's the connection between the dead guy and you?'

I considered. 'Almost none. No paper. One call to his answering machine. Good chance he wiped it.'

'What if he didn't?'

'Then they'll contact me, but you're still in the clear.'

'What's going on, Cliff?'

I was wound tight and hadn't realised it. My head was throbbing where Wain had hit me and the scab on my lip felt like a tumour. I let out a slow breath. 'I'm tempted to say the less you know the better, but I have a feeling you wouldn't like that.'

'Damn right.'

I filled him in as fully as I could. The talking did my nerves some good and helped to order my thoughts. Hank is a quick study.

'You figure this guy Sawtell got wind of you and Mrs Heysen looking into the doc's history and thought he had to do something about it.'

'Right. My guess is that Cassidy and Wain covered for him way back. He probably paid them pretty well. Wain was on the skids and when I told him what I was doing he saw a chance to get some more money out of Sawtell. But by all accounts Sawtell is as smart as they come. He played Wain along, sort of offered him a contract on Catherine Heysen and me. But Wain wasn't up to it.'

'So Sawtell eliminated him.'

'It's a lot of guesswork but it fits.'

Hank took a packet of chewing gum from his pocket and offered it to me. I refused. He started chewing. 'Helps me to think,' he said.

'About what?'

'About how you and the woman are still targets. Maybe more than ever. What about the son, this William? He in it?'

'I don't see how. He's a side issue.'

'I figure I've still got the job of watching your back.'

'Not immediately, mate. I'm going to lay low. See if the cops come after me. If they do I'll tell them what I've told

you and they can make of it what they will. They won't like
me walking away, but they can't tag me for it. I haven't fired
a gun in months. Anyway, it wasn't a .38 that made that
splatter.'

Hank chewed rhythmically and was silent for a few long
minutes. 'I guess he was no great loss, Wain.'

'Not much. He was in a bad slide. In a way, Sawtell, if
that's who it was, did him a favour.'

That's how we left it. I told Hank I'd contact him when
I needed him. I phoned in the news of the dead body from
somewhere in Chippendale and went home.

Wain's death barely made the newspapers. Nothing on TV.
I phoned Frank to put him in the picture. I gave him an
outline.

'Better thrash it out in person,' he said.

He invited me to the get-together to welcome Peter and
his wife, as she now was, home. I'm Peter's anti-godfather,
but about all I've ever done for him, apart from birthday
presents when he was younger, was teach him to surf.
I reckon that was a gift for life.

I kept a close lookout on the drive to Paddington and
I was sure I wasn't followed. I went into the house where
Hilde was waiting nervously, fiddling with a flower arrange-
ment.

'Frank's collecting them from the airport. What if she
doesn't like us?' she said.

'You've already met her. You said she did.'

'I thought she did.'

'Don't worry. You're quite likeable.'

'Here they are.'

Then it was all handshakes, kisses and champagne. I'd got Peter and Ramona a five hundred dollar David Jones voucher as a wedding present. Not inspired, but useful.

Peter was a carbon copy of his father, a bit taller and with a full head of dark hair that would probably turn grey like Frank's. He was bearded and very tanned from his time in South America. He had an easy, poised manner, a bit self-deprecating. Ramona was a relaxed, confident young woman, not exactly beautiful but all the more attractive for that. Peter clearly adored her and it wasn't hard to see why.

Hilde had laid on a spread and we all hopped into it.

'Where's this Lily I've heard about?' Peter asked me.

'Working. You'll meet her sooner or later.'

'Good. This is all a bit weird, Cliff. Coming back to the totally familiar surroundings with a wife and twins on the way and hearing of this brother. Dad told me about it. It's a lot for Mum to cope with.'

'She'll manage. Life is immense, as Manning Clark said. I think it was Manning Clark.'

'Sounds like him. Dad says you're not too keen on him, this William.'

'I think he's a prick and he could be headed for big trouble. I just don't want it to rub off on Frank.'

'You look pretty beat up. That's nothing new but you seem stressed as well. What else is going on?'

'Not your problem, mate. You've got enough on your plate.'

Hilde had downed a few glasses and was getting expansive. She shoved Peter aside and put her arm around me. 'You were right,' she said. 'I shouldn't have worried. She's great, isn't she?'

'Yep. Lucky boy. Reckon they'll settle here?'

Hilde laughed. 'Peter, settle? No chance. He'll probably be off to help the tsunami generation and she'll go too, with the babies on her back. They're two of a kind.'

Frank grabbed a half-full bottle and gestured at me to come into his study. We sat down. He poured.

'Tell me the rest of it,' he said.

I did, leaving nothing out. It was a second run-through on the theories and connections and it made it all more solid. For me.

'It's thin,' Frank said. 'Pity you didn't get to Wain first.'

'I imagine he'd agree with you.'

'He was a bit of a shit but you know how it is. You don't like to hear about a cop's past catching up with him. We've all got skeletons—look at me.'

'You haven't connived at helping a murdering corrupt police officer get away with everything he did. Think of the harm Cassidy and Wain must've done over the years. The Sawtell cover-up wouldn't be the only thing.'

'You're right there. If you're right about the rest of it I just can't understand why Sawtell would stick around. He'd be safer in Thailand or some place.'

'Maybe he went away and came back.'

As soon as I spoke the same thought struck us simultaneously. 'Jesus,' Frank said, 'didn't William tell you he was into an immigration racket—passports, documents, all that?'

I nodded. 'That's a big jump, Frank.'

Frank drained his glass. 'You started it. Sawtell's in Indonesia, say, sitting pretty. William Heysen comes in sniffing around looking to make money with an immigration scam. Sawtell's already screwed his father for some reason or other and now it amuses him to get the son into deep shit. I told you he was devious and vicious.'

'With a sense of humour.'

'Right. Twisted, though, and directed at other people rather than himself. He's capable of just about anything you can think of. If that kid's in with him he's in trouble.'

'He's not your responsibility. There've been so many lies and so much deception.'

'I feel that he is, but it's more than that. Sawtell's a danger to Catherine, you, me, William, everybody.'

'I think I can find William,' I said.

'You didn't tell me that.'

I was a bit drunk; I waved my glass. 'With all this fun we're having it must've slipped my mind.'

21

I went for a long walk around Paddington and Darlinghurst. I passed the block of flats where Roma Brown lived and couldn't help looking up at the window opposite where she saw things that stimulated her. Nothing to see from street level. The ground floor of the building that had housed the Heysen–Bellamy medical practice had become some kind of IT consultancy. Sign of the times.

The food had blotted up some of the alcohol, and after I drank coffee back at Frank and Hilde's place I was fit to drive home. Lily was there, picking up things she hadn't yet collected. I hadn't seen her for a few days but that was nothing unusual. I'd phoned but got her answering machine three times, which meant that she was hard at work. We fell back into comfortable dealings very easily.

'You've been on the piss,' she said. She touched my lip where the split was knitting into a pale scar. 'Don't tell me you did that falling over.'

'That's an honourable professional wound.'

'One of many.'

I told her about Peter and Ramona and that they were

keen to meet her. I also told her about the confirmation that Frank was William Heysen's father.

'Interesting. I feel a bit out of it with all these stray kids turning up.'

'No you don't.'

She laughed. 'You're right. I'd be the mother from hell. Came close a few times but always had the scrape. I have to run, Cliff. Deadline. Give me a ring. Always glad to see Frank and Hilde.'

'Grandpa and Grandma to be.'

She kissed me and left.

My contact at the RTA had read too much le Carré and Len Deighton. He liked to think of himself as a mole, selling his organisation's secrets to an enemy power. In a way he's right, and he is taking risks, although the worst he'd get is dismissal rather than the Lubianka or the Isle of Wight. Still, that's the way he likes to play it. My payment goes into his TAB account which, since he charges steeply and I'm sure I'm not his only client, perhaps suggests why he keeps on working.

I phoned him with William Heysen's car registration number.

'I'm snowed under,' he said. 'Call you back.'

'It's urgent.'

'It'll cost you.'

'What first-class service doesn't?'

That got me a laugh and a pretty quick return call. William Franz Heysen drove a late model Toyota Land Cruiser—colour black. His address was 2/15 Shetland Street, Bowral.

'You sure about that?'

'Checks with the driver's licence. I threw that in for free. You want the previous addresses on the licence? Cost you extra.'

'No, thanks.'

'Roger.' He named the fee. 'Over and out.' Maybe he'd been a Biggles reader.

I hadn't seen William as a country dweller but then, maybe Bowral isn't exactly country these days. All I knew about it was that Graham Kennedy had lived there somewhere before he died, and that Jimmy Barnes once had a place there too. Maybe still did.

I was about to pick up the phone to tell Frank I had an address for William when it rang.

'Mr Hardy, you've been neglecting me.'

Catherine Heysen was one of those people who didn't feel the need to identify themselves over the phone, believing that they can project themselves sufficiently by voice alone. With her, it worked.

'I'm sorry, Mrs Heysen. There's been quite a lot going on.'

'Which I want to hear about. I suppose you've seen Frank and know his paternity has been confirmed.'

'Yes.'

'Have you found where William is?'

'Sort of.'

'We really must talk. I'd like you to come here, please. After all, I am paying you.'

She couldn't resist slipping that in, but she had a point. There was a fair bit to tell her and, as Frank had said, she was still in danger if our theories were right. William could wait. But I wasn't going to let her have it all her own way.

'How's the shoulder?'

'Healing very well, thank you.'

Almost flirtatious at first, she was now back to being the ice queen. William had said she was a liar and had dropped other hints about her, but there was no good reason to believe that he always told the truth. I'm amused whenever I hear someone say, 'I like working with people'. People are hell.

'Mr Hardy?'

'I could be there in an hour.'

She'd got what she wanted. She hung up without another word.

I always think Lane Cove has a look of mortgages having been paid off. I'm not sure why, it probably isn't true, but the suburb has a comfortable feel, as if the residents have put their troubles to rest. The house where Catherine Heysen was staying was more comfortable than most—an expansive Federation number that had been given another storey without too much disturbance of its original lines. Hard to do. It was set on a big sloping block so that the house was well above the street level and would have, from the upper floor, a good view over the houses opposite to the National Park. Might even catch a glimpse of the river.

No need to worry about security. A high cyclone fence overgrown with creeper ran along the side, and both gates in the imposing brick fence had all the alarm systems they needed. I pressed a buzzer by the entrance, aware that I was under video surveillance. After a short pause the heavy iron gate swung open and I went up a tiled path to the house. Wide verandahs all around. Well-tended garden on both sides, well-worn bluestone steps.

The door opened before I reached it and a largish man in a suit stood waiting for me. He stuck out his hand. Heavy rings on two fingers. Had to be the brother who took after the mum.

'Bruno Beddoes,' he said. 'Catherine's brother.'

It struck me that this was how William Heysen might look in twenty years time—confident, well-groomed, a bit soft. That's if he managed to stay out of gaol in one country or another. We shook hands and he told me that Catherine was waiting for me at the back. We went down a wide hallway with rooms off either side to a short passage leading out through French doors to the verandah. More tiles, more creeper, hanging baskets, wind chimes.

Catherine Heysen was posed on a cane lounge with a cashmere blanket over her knees. She wore a loose black sweater which emphasised her pallor. Wearing less makeup but with her hair carefully arranged, she had an air of fragility quite unlike how she had appeared at our first meeting. She extended her hand to me and I took it briefly. Cool and dry. What else?

'Please sit down, Mr Hardy. Would you like some tea or coffee? Perhaps a drink?'

'Nothing, thank you. I can't stay long. I've found that your son is living in Bowral. I'm driving down there this evening to talk to him. He's apparently involved in some-thing that could land him in trouble. Frank's very concerned about him.'

'As I'd expect. What sort of trouble?'

'To do with immigration as I told you. The details are unclear.'

'Surely there's legitimate work in that area?'

'I suppose so, but the indications are . . .'

'And what are they, the indications?'

'Can I tell you the suspicions I have about who may have framed your husband and arranged for you to be shot?'

'You already have—a disgruntled client of Gregory's to do with his . . . unpleasant sideline. I found it plausible.'

She couldn't help patronising me, just couldn't hold it in. I remembered Lily saying she would have been the mother from hell. This woman looked more like it. I tossed up whether to tell her almost nothing or to hit her right between the eyes. Pique won out.

'There's a man named Matthew Henry Sawtell. He—'

The almond eyes flashed and her clasped hands flew up to her face. 'Oh, my God!'

Better than I thought, but too much better. She stared at me through her fingers.

'I . . . I knew him,' she said. 'I thought he was dead.'

'He might be, or he might not. I told you this was just a suspicion.'

She was genuinely alarmed and, although I doubted the genuineness of her invalid pose, she had been shot and could still be emotionally shaky. I half rose from my seat.

'Are you all right? Can I get you something?'

'Yes, yes please. Can you find someone in the house and ask them to get me a cognac.'

Make it two, I thought.

When I arrived the house had seemed empty, apart from Bruno, but now people appeared from everywhere. Another man and two women. The women fussed over Catherine and Bruno produced a bottle of cognac and a couple of glasses. He handed me the tray.

'I hope you're not upsetting her.'

'Trying not to, but I think some chickens are coming home to roost.'

'What the hell does that mean?'

'You can ask her when I go.'

'Make that soon.'

I went back to the verandah and poured two solid drinks. She tossed off half of hers and then took a small sip as she looked at a point somewhere above my head.

'Matthew Sawtell and I were lovers. I . . . left him for Frank.'

I was tempted to tell her that William had said she had a thing for uniforms, but I kept quiet.

Speaking slowly, she went on. 'He was very upset about it. Frank was junior to him and it hurt his pride. Of course he was married. He was in no position to—'

'Did Frank know of your relationship with Sawtell?'

'No, because Matthew was married we kept it very secret.'

It was a whole new element but it didn't disturb the theory, rather it strengthened it. If Sawtell had a grudge against Heysen, presumably for making a mess of the plastic job, he'd be pleased to get back at the woman who'd dumped him as well. I didn't need to spell it out for her. She finished her drink and held out the glass for more. I obliged. This was the closest to loss of control that I'd seen in her and she couldn't hold back.

'I haven't been entirely truthful with you, or with Frank. It was true that I thought Frank could be William's father and that's how it turned out. And I didn't think Gregory would behave as the police said he did. But my real reason for contacting Frank was that . . . I needed someone, I wanted him . . .'

More cognac went down and I had some myself. Good stuff.

'I've had an empty life since coming back from Italy. I hate it here and only stayed for William's sake. If we'd remained in Italy he would have had to do military service and who knows what might have happened to him? And after all that, and trying to be a good mother, everything fell apart. I needed someone. Do you understand?'

I did, but I didn't entirely believe her. She was capable of being more than just economical with the truth, she could adjust it to suit her needs and probably believed the adjustment was the reality. Behind that beautiful face was a disturbed psyche. I was sure she'd manipulated William from the cradle on. She had the knack, as shown by the kind of treatment she was getting in this house. I gave her no more than a semi-encouraging nod.

'And Frank didn't want me, of course. Why would he? He had a wife and a child, people he loved. And he handed the problem on to you. And now I . . .'

She would always circle back to herself from whatever point she started. She stopped speaking, took another belt of the cognac and then the thought got to her, through the protective shield of her self-concern.

'My God,' she said, 'you don't think William is involved with Matthew Sawtell?'

She was one of those people who go easy on themselves and blame others. I didn't spare her. 'Why not?' I said.

'He's a murderer.'

'Yes, and if all this speculation's right, he's already killed a man just recently.'

'Who?'

'The man who shot you and bashed me.'

Her hand trembled as she put the glass down on the tiles. 'I didn't know what I was doing.'

'That's right,' I said, 'you didn't.'

Big Bruno tried to block me on my way out but I was moving quickly; I caught him by surprise and pushed him aside.

'Look after her,' I said. 'She seems to be upset.'

22

Outside it was dark with a chill wind getting up. I sat in the car grateful for its warmth and tried to think about what to do next. There were things to tell Frank but nothing he'd want to hear. I thought about how matters had fallen into place for him—Hilde, Peter, his grandchildren on the way. Leave him in peace, I thought. Against that, if it was really Sawtell we were up against, and he went feral, that peace could be shattered. I couldn't decide. Army strategy seemed like the best bet—when in doubt, do a recce.

I keep the necessities for operational survival—toothbrush, razor, soap, towel, a half-bottle of whisky and two plastic containers, one full of water, the other to piss in—in the car. The downside of my arrangement with Lily is the frequent lonely nights, the upside is not having to check in.

I worked my way south-west, picked up the freeway and followed it down as it skirted towns like Yerrinbool and Mittagong. Time was when you had to go through them and country driving was like driving in the country. Now it's set the cruise control and get there, not that the Falcon has cruise control. I turned on the radio to catch the news.

Just in case Bush had pressed the button and this was all a waste of time.

As I drove I wondered whether I still had a client. Catherine Heysen had bared her soul. More than anything else she'd been man-hunting. I had to assume she still cared for her son but, given her egocentricity, that was a slender thread and my rudeness to her might have been enough to snap it. Possibly, but probably not. As for Frank, whose money I still hadn't worked through, he'd be pissed off at this independent action. But I could always mend bridges with him. That led to the thought that my objective here, for both parties, was to get William Heysen clear of the shit.

It was after 9 pm when I reached Bowral but the town hadn't closed down. Several pubs were busy and there were restaurants doing fair to good business along the main street. The days when all you'd find in a town like this was a Greek cafe, maybe a Chinese, were long gone. Good thing.

I was low on petrol and energy and I pulled in at a servo with a fast food outfall, as Andrew Denton had once styled them. I topped up, bought a street map of the town, coffee, and the least toxic-looking sandwich I could see in the display case. I sat in the far corner of the sparsely populated eating area, concealed the action behind the map, and spiked the coffee with cut-price scotch. Maybe it was just my hunger, or the alcohol lift or my hyped-up state, but the sandwich tasted surprisingly good and I bought another.

No problem locating Shetland Street; it ran off the main drag, not far from where I was. A short cul-de-sac. I wouldn't have expected William to locate himself in the foothills. I ate the second sandwich, drank the coffee and speculated about the town. All the signs were that it was keeping pace with the times: the restaurants and cafes, the craft shops—all with advertised websites—bricked footpaths and judiciously spaced and nicely staked trees. It undoubtedly had computer service companies and broadband. Many of the houses I'd seen on the way in had sprouted pay-TV satellite dishes. A good place to set up William's probably dodgy operation—good communications, close enough, but not too close rent-wise to Sydney and Canberra. A good place for 'Mad Matt' Sawtell to ply whatever trade he was pursuing?

The payphone in the service station cafe had a phone book and I looked up William. No listing. Without any particular plan in mind, I drove to Shetland Street. William's flat was in a new and pretty up-market block above a collection of four shops. The street was well lit and I could see that the complex had high security—an electronically controlled gate to get to the parking area and something similar at the foot entrance.

I got out of the car and crossed the street for a closer inspection. There were four apartments. You had to buzz to get past the gate and there were no names posted. I buzzed all four: two didn't answer and the two that responded did so with female voices. A girlfriend? Didn't seem likely. Neither voice sounded young. Presumably our boy was out somewhere. Well, I could wait.

I took a look at the shops: a Vietnamese bakery, an accountant, a hair and beauty pit stop, and a travel agency—Speciality Travel. A sign in the smoked glass window read: 'passport photographs, visas arranged, online bookings, video conferencing'. No way to be sure, but it looked as if William could be cutting down the time and distance between home and work.

I made a mental note of Speciality Travel's phone number and webpage address and went back to the car to jot them down. I was settled with notebook and pen in hand when I felt the cold bite of metal at the base of my skull.

'Drop the stuff in your hands and put them on the wheel. High up—five to one.'

The instruction came with a sharp jab and then an easing of the pressure. Someone who knew what he was doing.

I dropped the pen and notebook and did as I'd been told. I glanced at the rear vision mirror but it had been moved so that it showed nothing immediately behind me. A true professional.

'You don't have to look, you just have to listen,' the voice said. 'This is a sawn-off pump action shotgun with a heavy load. If you don't do what I say, exactly what I say, your head disappears.'

The sweat broke out immediately—on my body, on my face, on my hands—the voice and the threat had that much conviction. My throat was suddenly too dry to let me speak. I coughed and cleared it.

'Sawtell?'

Another quick jab and then something was hanging from my right ear.

'Plastic restraint,' he said. 'Right hand up and fasten it to your right wrist and the steering wheel.'

'I might need two hands for that.'

'Use them while you've got them.'

His calm was unnerving. I could only just hear him breathing, nothing heavy or out of rhythm. I adjusted the restraint, but left the clasp loose.

'Give it a tug.'

He had me. I closed the clasp and tugged.

'Okay. Marks for a good try. Now I think we can relax a bit. Or at least I can.'

'You can't ever relax, not to the end of your days.'

'True. For now, I mean. I knew you'd turn up here sooner or later, Hardy. How'd you do it? Did bright boy Willy let you see his car?'

'Figure it out.'

'Doesn't matter. I was told you knew your business and I had a man keep an eye on you.'

'Like Rex Wain?'

'Better, a bit better at least. Not hard.'

'I suppose they'll be expendable too.'

The shotgun barrel rapped sharply against my ear, drawing blood.

'This isn't a debating society. I'm going to tell you what you're going to do.'

'Or?'

'Or everything ends for you right here.'

'Fuck you!'

'What?'

'You heard me. You're talking too much, Sawtell. You want something. You want it badly and you need me to get it for you. So spell it out and we'll see where it takes us. But you're not going to blow my head off until you're sure you can't use me. So, as I say, fuck you.'

'You've got guts, I'll say that for you.'

The sweat was dripping from me and I'd played him as hard as I was ever going to be able to. It was time to ease up if I wanted to stay alive. He'd killed men before, some in hot blood, some in cold. He was as dangerous as a shark in bloody water.

'Tell me a few things,' I said. 'Indulge me professionally. Let's see where we get to.'

'You're a piece of work.'

That struck a false note—maybe he'd been watching too much television, had too much time on his hands. I was tempted to tell him so but I resisted, thinking I'd probably pushed him far enough. I kept quiet, forcing him to speak again.

'So what d'you want to know?'

'Did you frame Gregory Heysen?'

'Yes.'

'Why?'

'No comment. Anything else?'

'My guess is you ran into William Heysen somewhere in South-East Asia. Let's say Indonesia.'

'Close. Singapore.'

'You encouraged him to go into what he calls immigration facilitation, better known as people-smuggling.'

'He was willing.'

'Again, why?'

'Same answer. That's enough, but in case you're wondering, you won't find him across the street there. He's somewhere else.'

'Forced restraint's a serious charge.'

'Don't make me laugh. I've got two murder counts on the sheet.'

'Plus Wain.'

'Shut up and listen. You get me what I want or I'll send the little smartarse to you in pieces. Don't think I don't mean it.'

It had to be something to do with Dr Gregory Heysen again. Some retribution. I considered telling him Heysen wasn't William's father, but I couldn't see what good it would do at that moment. Maybe later.

'I'm listening.'

'I want to see Catherine.'

So it was all circling back towards her. I knew there was no point in asking him why. There was only one sensible thing to ask.

'How? You had her shot. She's still recovering and very well protected.'

'I know that. It's something for you to figure out. You've worked a lot of stuff out so far, let's see how smart you really are.'

He opened the door and I felt a surge of alarm. 'You can't just—'

'Shook you then, didn't I? Tell me your mobile number. Don't think, just do it.'

I rattled the number off.

'Right. I'll be in touch. Sit tight and don't turn round. If I see you move I'll blast the back of the car and let you take your chances with glass and the petrol tank.'

Opening the door had turned on the interior light. I was a big, well-lit target. I heard him slide out and I didn't move a muscle.

23

I'd been overconfident, or let's call it what it was—slack again. Hank Bachelor hadn't been immediately available to watch my back and I'd let that precaution slip. I was sure I hadn't been followed all the way from where Catherine Heysen was staying, but I'd been picked up there by someone communicating with Sawtell and once I was on the highway to the Southern Highlands that would be all he needed. A good tail is hard to spot in suburban traffic, much easier on the freeways.

I sat in the car feeling diminished and furious with myself. Pointless, and the game wasn't over yet by a long shot. Sawtell had expressed a need, always a weakness. And I knew at least one or two things he didn't know. I scrabbled in my jacket pocket for my Swiss army knife, got it open and sawed through the plastic restraint where it circled my wrist. I left it hanging on the steering wheel as a reminder of the mistake I'd made.

It wasn't late and I found an open motel in Bowral. Didn't make the same mistake twice; I was sure I hadn't been followed. I checked in and parked myself at the desk with a scotch and a packet of nuts from the mini-bar and jotted down all I could remember of what was said in the confrontation with Sawtell. Wrong word. I hadn't seen him. He'd taken steps to avoid that. I noted the fact and added a large question mark. I finished the scotch and opened another of the miniature bottles, adding soda this time. I cracked open the packet of crisps and ate them as I continued making notes. When I scrunched up the packet to drop it into the bin I was surprised to see that they were salt and vinegar flavoured. I hadn't even tasted them. Good sign that I was concentrating on the problems at hand.

There were enough. Sawtell implied he had William Heysen under control. A good bargaining chip in his wish to see Catherine Heysen. I was evidently to be the go-between, not a comfortable role. It all raised the question of whether and when to bring Frank in. The hostage was his son and he felt responsible for him although they'd never met. Or had they? Had Frank interviewed Catherine when her husband was being investigated? Had he seen the baby? Did it matter?

I decided that my tired brain was scrambling things and that it was time to give it a rest. I finished the drink, cleaned my teeth and crawled naked into bed. Before I went to sleep I had a mildly comforting thought: hostage-takers might seem to have the right of way, but they don't succeed all that often. They're actually in a two-way street. And there was absolutely no way to predict how Catherine Heysen would react.

I'm not one of those people who can only sleep in his own bed. For me a bed's a bed, and if I'm tired enough I can sleep in it. The encounter with Sawtell had been tiring in the sense that giving a lecture is or getting up to sing a few songs—not much physical effort and doesn't take long, but it's draining. I slept soundly and if I dreamed I didn't remember any of them when I woke up.

I started the day with a cup of the motel's instant coffee—two sachets plus whitener. I shaved and showered and decided yesterday's shirt would do again. I lazed around until business hours and then drove to Shetland Street. The bread shop was trading, the accountant had his sign out and there was activity inside Lucia's, the beauty parlour. Speciality Travel was shut up tight.

I went into Lucia's and asked the young woman arranging things under a five metre long mirror if she knew what time the travel agency opened. She flicked back the sleeve of her pink smock and looked at her watch.

'Should be open by now. Hey, Karen, what time does Will open?'

Another woman, also young and perfectly turned out with the hair, the smock, the nails, poked her head through a curtain.

'Nine thirty,' she said, 'but I haven't seen him for a couple of days. Must be sick.'

The woman I'd spoken to first shrugged. 'I'm part-time.'

'You know him though.'

'Well. . .' She stopped what she was doing to take a proper look at me. I was presentable, I thought, just, but people's standards vary. 'Why do you ask?'

Good question. I gave her a card that said who I was and what I did.

'Ooh, is Will in trouble?'

'Not from me. Maybe from someone else. I'm working

for his mother. I can give you her number if you want to check that.'

She did a nice line in shrugs. 'No. There's nothing much I can tell you. I cut his hair last week. Trimmed it, really.'

'I didn't think this was a unisex place.'

'The world is a unisex place.'

I laughed and she smiled. 'I saw that on TV. You gave me the opening.'

'You did it well. So he hasn't been around for a few days?'

'So Karen says. She'd know.'

'How was he when you saw him?'

'Sweet but, you know, a bit up himself.'

'That's him.'

Karen came out from behind the curtain, apparently keen not to miss anything. 'Something wrong, Trish?'

Trish showed her my card. She wasn't impressed—maybe it was my hair. I asked when she'd last seen William and she said four days ago. I asked if his business seemed to be going well.

'Hard to say,' Karen said. 'People come and go—foreigners, you know, like Asians and Arabs and that.'

'No Caucasians?'

'What?'

'White people.'

'Not many. There was this one guy . . .'

'Yes?'

She put her perfectly manicured hand up to her smooth cheek. 'I called him Scarface. Real ugly, a real mess. Should've seen a plastic surgeon. He drove a cool black Beemer so he must have the money. Trish, get busy, Mrs Turnbull's due any minute.'

'Does he live here, this bloke with the scarred face? Have you ever seen him around the town?'

Karen shook her head. 'No.'

That was all I was going to get. I thanked them and left.

I enquired at the accountant's office and got nothing at all—professional discretion. I stared longingly at Speciality Travel's locked door and the apartments above and behind, but there was no way of broaching them.

As I moved back to my car, a man wearing a turban approached the travel agency door. I went across to him non-threateningly, and spoke as politely as I could.

'Excuse me, are you here to see Mr Heysen?'

He didn't like the look of me one bit. 'Sorry, sorry,' he said and hurried off, almost tripping on the gutter.

I couldn't see what else there was to be done in Bowral. Maybe Sawtell was holed up here, maybe not. I didn't fancy asking around for Scarface and his Beemer. The day had dawned grey all around, and the wind was keen. Southern Highlands after all, have to expect that. The only thing to do was head back to the city: Catherine Heysen was the key to the next moves and it was definitely time to bring Frank in—to disturb his peace of mind. After experiencing the hard-line resourcefulness of Sawtell, I felt the need for backup such as Frank and Hank Bachelor could provide. Still, I did a run up and down the main street and a few cross streets and out to a couple of housing estates and the business park, looking for a cool black BMW. Waste of effort.

Conference time. When I got back to the city I phoned Hank and brought him up to date on the essentials. He said the earliest he could make a meeting was five o'clock. Frank wasn't at home. I phoned Lily and got her to pull some strings. A couple of hours later the fax, not used that much these days, sparked up and copies of news clippings from the *Sydney Morning Herald*, the *National Times* and the *Sun* began to come through. The cuttings covered the trial, conviction and escape of Matthew Henry Sawtell.

He was born in Balmain, had just enough education to make it into the Police Academy, and was considered an outstanding recruit. Tall, strongly built and athletic, he impressed all the right people, did well in uniform with a couple of citations for bravery, and rose quickly as a detective. After his fall investigative journalists working on the story discovered family connections to the Painters and Dockers and signs that Sawtell had never seen the police force as anything other than a means of personal enrichment. He wore the livid scar on his face as a badge of honour. There were several photographs of him, mostly wearing a hat. Grainy and blotchy though the faxes were, his strong, almost handsome features were apparent. In one photo taken when he was a young man, before he got the scar, Herb Elliot's arm was around his shoulders. Catherine Heysen's kind of guy.

I got through to Frank in the mid-afternoon, told him most of what was going on, and he agreed to the five o'clock meeting in my office. I sat and waited for them with my mobile on the desk. I dislike the things, the fiddly little buttons, the dopey ring-tones, the expectation they've set up that unless you have one you're not a serious player at anything from shopping to international diplomacy. No choice now—it was the only connection to Mad Matt 'Scarface' Sawtell. He didn't need to have anyone keeping tabs on me now. From his point of view he had me where he wanted me. The trick would be to turn that around.

Hank got there first. He settled in a chair and surprised me by lighting a cigarette.

'Stress,' he said.

I nodded. I got an ashtray from the desk drawer, produced my emergency ration scotch and poured him a drink in a paper cup. He took it and nursed it gratefully. The chair I'd set out for Frank was one I'd found in an empty office in the building—I don't do much conferencing.

Frank arrived looking anxious. He accepted a drink before glancing around the office. It was his first time there.

'Shit, Cliff, can't you afford something better than this?'

'Low overhead. Money spent on essentials.'

'Yeah, like a good car.'

'What's got up your nose?'

'Sorry. Personal stuff. Let's get on with it. I admit I'm pissed off about you going after William without telling me. What did you plan to say to him?'

I shrugged. 'I was going to play it by ear. Find out if he was hooked up with Sawtell and try to talk him out of it.'

Hank said, 'That doesn't matter now. What d'we do when he makes contact and expects you to set up a meeting with Mrs Heysen?'

Frank shook his head. 'Can't let that happen.'

'What do you suggest?' I said. 'Give it to the police?'

I could almost see Frank's brain cells working. Playing by the book, he shouldn't have any involvement in this given his relationship to one of the pawns in the game, or two of them—three if you counted Sawtell. Too close to too much. But the police record in hostage bargaining situations is 50/50 at best and there were other considerations.

Sawtell was an experienced shooter facing a never-to-be-released label if caught. With nothing to lose he'd kill if pushed into a corner and take as many with him as he felt like.

'No,' Frank said. 'He expressed his hatred for the police at his trial and I don't imagine he's changed.'

'Cassidy and Wain are out of the picture,' I said, 'but some of the people who helped him escape could still be around and wouldn't want him talking. Remember our feelings along those lines when I got pulled by those two Ds? It only takes a spark to set off a hostage situation.'

'What?' Hank said.

I opened my hands. 'Sorry, mate. Wheels within wheels. There're probably cops and others who don't want him around.'

Hank didn't take offence, one of his strengths. 'Okay, we know he's got some helpers,' Hank said. 'What I can't understand is why he wants to see Mrs Heysen. Why he's back here at all.'

'They were lovers,' I said.

Hank took his cigarette pack out, glanced at Frank and put it away. 'So? Ancient history.'

'It doesn't feel that ancient,' Frank said.

I'd hardly touched my drink. Now I took a sip. 'At least we can be sure Heysen did the operation on Sawtell and botched it. Sawtell got away but he was a good-looking guy whose face was ruined. He took revenge on Heysen. But Hank's question remains.'

We sat there with no answers. Then my mobile rang.

24

'Don't answer it,' Frank said.

Hank stared at him.

'String him along for a bit. Don't give him the high ground.'

The phone rang for a while, then stopped. Hank nodded. 'Guess you've been in this kind of situation before. First time for me.'

'Not exactly,' Frank said, 'but there are certain principles, right, Cliff?'

'That's right,' I said. 'The trouble is they change with the circumstances.'

Hank shook his head. 'That means they're not principles. Let's say a principle is we don't let Sawtell meet with Mrs Heysen. Will that hold for all circumstances?'

'Yes,' Frank said.

'Then how does anything happen?'

Frank looked at me. 'Remember the Patterson siege?'

I did. Wilbur Patterson was a serial killer who'd holed up in his mother's house with his father as a hostage. He wanted to meet with his girlfriend and the police had no doubt he'd kill her and his father.

'It was before your time here, Hank.' I gave him the essentials.

'So what went down?'

'We used a stand-in for the girlfriend,' Frank said.

'How'd it come out?'

'Pretty good—the father wounded, the stand-in unharmed, Patterson dead.'

'A win.'

Frank took a sip of his drink. 'We were lucky. Patterson had poor eyesight and he panicked.'

'Doesn't sound like this Sawtell's the panicky type.'

'No,' I said. 'But he must be under pressure of some kind or he wouldn't be into this. What worries me is a feeling I have that he doesn't care whether he comes out of it alive or not. That's about as bad as it gets in these things.'

The phone rang again. Frank looked at his watch and shook his head. 'Next time.'

'What if he changes his mind?' Hank said. 'Cuts his losses. We don't know where he is. He's home free.'

'That's not Sawtell,' Frank said. 'He does what he says he'll do.'

'How'd he get caught then?'

I'd read the cuttings and could answer that. 'He trusted two people he shouldn't have.'

'So he's a poor judge of character?'

I nudged the mobile with a pen, just to be doing something. 'Aren't we all.'

The phone rang again and I picked it up.

'Hardy.'

'You're in your office in Newtown. You have two men with you. One's vaguely familiar but I can't place him. I don't know the other one.'

'They'd love to meet you,' I said.

'I bet. I wonder if they'd like to meet the shottie.'

'They'd cope.' I scribbled a note to Hank. He read it and was on his way instantly. 'How're you coping, Sawtell? I spoke to a woman who saw you at William's travel place. She wasn't attracted.'

He laughed. 'You'd be surprised how many are. Like I said, I want to see Catherine.'

Frank was at my elbow and I scribbled the gist of what Sawtell was saying.

'Well, I suppose that might be possible. She'd need to know that William was safe.'

'Fair enough. I'd let her talk to him and instruct my little helper to let him go when I was satisfied.'

'What would satisfy you?'

'Wait and see.'

'We'd need a bit more than that.'

'So would I, like a clear passage out. Who's that with you? I can tell you're communicating.'

I wrote: 'Wants a getaway route. Who're you?'

Frank took the phone. 'This is Frank Parker, Sawtell. Remember me?'

I didn't hear Sawtell's response but he must have asked what rank Frank had achieved because Frank said, 'Deputy commissioner.'

Frank took over the scribbling role and wrote: 'Two birds, one stone'.

He said, 'What does that mean?'

'No police—William dead', he wrote.

'I hear you,' Frank said. 'Like to tell me why you're doing this?'

Frank sat with the phone in his hand, evidently with nothing coming through it. 'Sawtell?'

Then Frank waved the phone in the air, indicating that the call was finished. The last words he'd written were 'three hours'.

'What?' I said.

'Three hours to set it up. He'll call again with the arrangement.'

'It's hard to follow a two-way conversation from notes. Did you . . . pick up anything useful? Apart from what the bastard wants?'

Frank was silent and I had to prompt him. 'Frank?'

'I'm thinking. What did you pick up?'

I asked him about the two birds with one stone remark. He nodded. 'Means he knows Catherine dumped him for me.'

'The idea is to kill two birds with one stone, isn't it?'

'Right.'

'The only other bit I got was a funny thing he said. He referred to his little helper. How about you?'

'Nothing. A bit of hesitation when I asked him why he was doing it. He called me Mr Clean.'

Frank went back to his chair and drained his paper cup. All of a sudden he looked old and strained again, the way he had when this whole thing started. He pushed the cup towards me. 'Any more of that rotgut on hand?'

I poured him another slug and some for myself. It wasn't the answer to the fix we were in, but sometimes when you run out of ideas it seems like the only thing to do. It didn't look good for William and I thought about that as I sipped the drink. I hadn't liked him and could spare him, but then, I didn't like his mother either. Shouldn't matter, she was my client—or was she still? Very different for Frank—an old lover and a new son. No wonder he was feeling the strain.

I was about to say something just to break the silence when the desk phone rang.

'Cliff,' Hank Bachelor said. 'I got him. Would you believe he's driving that Commodore clunker?'

I mouthed Hank's name to Frank. 'That was careless.'

'Yeah. You'll never guess where he's gone.'

'Hank, Sawtell's given us three hours. No time for guessing games. Tell us.'

'Didn't you say Mrs Heysen lived in Earlwood? That's where we are. Big place near the river. Got a for sale sign out.'

I relayed this to Frank.

'That's crazy,' Frank said.

'What do you want me to do, Cliff?' Hank said.

'Has he gone into the house?'

'No, he's sitting in the car outside. Using his cell phone a bit.'

'Stay there. I'll get back to you. Did you see the driver?'

'Yeah, he stopped for smokes. Little guy.'

I hung up. 'Hank says he was small.'

'The little helper. This is weird. I can't imagine what he's playing at. It's crazy.'

'You said that already. Did he sound . . . unhinged to you?'

'No, but like I told you, he wouldn't, no matter what was going through his head.'

'One thing's clear—he's obsessed with the Heysens. Is there any way he'd know where Catherine is? Did her people live in Lane Cove back when Sawtell knew her?'

'No, Rockdale.'

'They stepped up. Let's assume he doesn't know where she is and can't check that she's not going anywhere. He only referred to one helper this time.'

'Well, he killed the other one.'

'Right. So he's at Earlwood with William and with one person in support. We outnumber them.'

'You're saying we go over there and do a Clint Eastwood?'

'It's a corner block. Easy access. Bachelor's got a stun gun and capsicum spray.'

Frank shook his head. 'I don't know.'

The only other option's to call in the police. My guess is Sawtell'd leave nobody standing. I think he is crazy, Frank. Mightn't show it, but what all this adds up to is last stand stuff.'

'You said . . . wrote, that he wanted a way out.'

'He's smart enough to fake that, isn't he?'

'Yes. Okay, we'll play it your way, but if it gets too sticky we go official. Where's your spare pistol?'

On the way I phoned Hank and told him to secure the man outside and call me back when he had. He did that within ten minutes.

'Name's Cassidy,' Hank said. 'Not much fight in him. I don't reckon his heart was in the job.'

I told this to Frank who was checking the .45 automatic I keep as backup. 'Cassidy had a son. Looks as if Sawtell had some leverage there.'

'Taking him out doesn't help us that much,' I said. 'We still have to get the jump on Sawtell. We need to talk to him. Tell him he's not going to see Catherine. Talk him out of harming William.'

'Tall order.'

'Are you willing to let him go?'

Frank said, 'I'm not sure. Let's see how it shapes up. Got any ideas about getting close?'

'One.'

I turned into the street and saw Hank's 4WD parked on the other side of the road and a little back from the red Commodore. I pulled in even further back and waved to Hank to join us. He trotted up looking pleased with himself.

'Where's Cassidy?' I said.

'He's in the trunk of his car. Says he has to check in with the guy in the house every forty-five minutes.' Hank looked at his watch. 'You've got about thirty.'

'What about weapons?'

'He didn't have anything. Guy in the house has a sawed-off and a handgun.'

'Okay,' I said. 'I've met the man in the house two up from the Heysen house. If he's there I think he'll let us go through his place. Then we can go over the fences and get in at the side. It's a corner block, as you see. I'm betting that if Sawtell's watching anywhere it'll be the other side and the back.'

Frank was wearing a suit. He stripped off the jacket and rolled up his sleeves. He put the .45 I'd given him in his pocket. Hank and I were in jeans, boots and T-shirts. I had a leather jacket and Hank a down-padded vest. He had his tazer on his belt and the capsicum spray in an inside pocket of the vest.

We went through the gate and up to the front of Professor Lowenstein's house. I hesitated for a second. He was an old man. How would he feel about this invasion? There was no time to spare. I rang the bell.

He came to the door and recognised me. 'Mr Hardy.'

I explained why we were there and he said he'd noticed

some activity at the Heysen house but assumed it was to do with the impending sale.

'We want to go through your back yard and the next one and see if we can resolve this with the element of surprise on our side.'

'Shouldn't the police—?'

'There isn't time, Professor,' I said.

Lowenstein wasn't a man to dither but he had his scruples. 'If it's a matter of time I'll allow you to do what you want but I'll call the police now. They'll take a while to get here. That's the best I can do.'

'Fair enough. What about your neighbour?'

'You're in luck there. An elderly couple, staying with their children for a time.'

We trooped through the house out to the back yard, which was showing signs of some neglect—overgrown flowerbeds and weeds breaking through the gravel paths. The fence to the next house was in poor repair and Hank had no trouble pulling a couple of palings free. We went through the yard and I didn't register a thing about it because I was concentrating on the next fence and what I could see of the Heysen house. It was a Colorbond job, newish and high. The shrubs in the Heysen property grew close to the fence along its length.

We moved up to the building line and Hank boosted first me and then Frank over the fence. Years younger than us, bigger and fitter, Hank easily hauled himself over it. We were crouched in a cluster of shrubs, three metres from the building line, ten from the door to the sunroom at the back. I gestured to Hank to move up beside the house. There were windows to the rooms along that side; the ground sloped but he was tall enough to be able to look in.

He came back crouching, and whispered, 'Kid's in the kitchen. Tied to a chair. Gagged with tape. No sign of the guy.'

A lot of our thirty minutes had elapsed. Sawtell would be expecting a call from his helper soon.

'Wish I had a flak jacket,' Hank said.

Frank said, 'Shut up!' He took the .45 from his pocket and dashed to the back door. He jerked at it, couldn't get it open, and kicked it three times so that the glass shattered. He reached in and released the lock.

'Sawtell!' Frank almost screamed.

I was close behind, swearing, sweating, and trying to get a good grip on my .38. I could hear Hank close behind me releasing the velcro on his hardware.

I lurched through the sunroom and stopped short, almost knocking Frank over. We were in the kitchen now and could see a thin, bald man sitting on the table, half turned towards us. His face was blotched and badly scarred and he held a pistol inches from William Heysen's right ear.

25

'Hello, Parker.'

'Sawtell.'

'I know Hardy. Who's the incredible hulk?'

'He's the one who put your little helper out of action,' I said.

'Not surprising. His father was pretty gutless if you remember, Parker.'

Frank went straight into hostage-with-armed-aggressor mode. Talk to them was the rule.

'How did you get the son to help you?' Frank said.

'Told him that if I revealed what I knew about his father that'd be the end of the mother's pension. Probably not true, but then he's not very bright.'

Buying time and following suit, I said, 'What about Wain?'

'Rex always came cheap.'

'Why'd you kill him?'

'Lost my temper. Simple as that.'

'Why here?' I said.

'I wanted to see where the bastard had lived—her too.'

'What's this all about, Sawtell?' Frank said. 'What d'you hope to gain?'

Sawtell shrugged and smiled. His face was truly horrible and the smile made it look worse. 'I guess you could say to make Catherine Beddoes suffer.'

'Why, because she dumped you?'

'No, no. Is that what she says? Bullshit. I gave her the flick in the end. Fish in the sea. You got to be deputy commissioner. Must be pretty smart or was it just arse-licking got you there? Can't you work it out?'

It was a bizarre situation, talking about old love affairs with a killer who held a couple of lives here and now in the palm of his hand. But talking was all there was to do.

'I'll have a guess,' I said. 'She knew her husband did plastic surgery. She steered you to him after your escape, but she told him you were her lover out of revenge for you dumping her. Heysen was insanely jealous and he botched the job on your face deliberately.'

'Pretty close. I got even with him through Padrone. Not with her though.'

William was in a bad way, pale, unshaven with his hair in a mess. His eyes were darting around and he was trembling. Sawtell held the pistol very steadily and there was no way for us to get closer. I wondered how far away the police were and how they'd react to what the professor told them. Would they come with sirens screaming?

'But you got clean away,' Frank said. 'You must have got your hands on the money you'd scammed when you were riding high.'

'Easy in those days. Yeah, and you can do all right in Singapore if you grease the right wheels. Squeaky clean on the outside, but you know how it is. Same the world over.'

'Why now, after all this time?'

Sawtell sighed and at that moment he looked old and

ill. 'I'd put it behind me. Got even with Heysen, like I said. Had good things going in Singapore. Then a couple of things happened. One, I got cancer, terminal. Two, I got sick of the place—wall to wall fucking slappies. I didn't want to die there. Pity that fucking tidal wave didn't come south and wash the place away. Shit, I represented this country in the Olympics. I had a right . . . Well, fuck that. Three, this little snotnose turned up—living image of her, making noises about getting into the immigration racket. Would you believe he carried a picture of her in a bikini in his wallet? Sick little bastard. I sucked him in and now I'm going to spit him out, unless you get fucking Catherine here so she can see what she did to me.'

'That's not going to happen,' Frank said.

'Then she's a childless widow, the poxy bitch. And I'll get a couple of you as well.'

Frank and I both had guns in our hands and Hank had unhooked his tazer.

'Not all,' Hank said. Brave, but his voice was shaky.

Sawtell's mutilated face lost expression and his pale eyes seemed to go blank. 'You think I care?'

A siren sounded briefly in the distance and Sawtell, the ex-policeman, couldn't stifle a small reaction. He swayed just slightly. William, the athlete, now fighting for his life, felt the minute change in the pressure. He threw his weight sideways and rocked the chair to a forty-five degree angle away from Sawtell.

Sawtell swore and fired. The bullet hit William and the impact threw him and the chair to the floor.

Frank shot Sawtell in the chest. Twice.

26

After that it was one big stink. Sawtell was dead and William had a serious leg wound. Hank went out to meet the cops that the professor had summoned, and to get them to call an ambulance. They gave him a bad time—stun guns are illegal for civilians. The kitchen was awash with blood from Sawtell and William. Frank untied William, used the rope to put a tourniquet on his leg, and slowed the bleeding down until the paramedics took over.

At that range, two .45 bullets, one dead centre in the chest and one lower left to the heart area, leave no doubt. Sawtell must have died within seconds of being hit.

The place filled with ambulance guys, uniformed police, detectives and scene-of-crime people, male and female. Frank and I identified ourselves and were held and cautioned. One of the detectives recognised Frank's name and treated him with a little more respect than he might have otherwise. Certainly more than Hank and I got. Frank told them who the dead man was and it didn't mean a thing to them. The police took possession of stuff Sawtell had in the house, including the sawn-off shotgun.

As we were being escorted to the police cars to be taken

to Surry Hills, Hank remembered Cassidy Junior in the boot of the Commodore. The police opened the boot and it was almost comical to see the relief on the small man's face. He put his hands in the air as though he was in a Western movie. But this wasn't the movies. None of us was handcuffed or manhandled. Our heads weren't thumped down as we were put in the cars. Frank was quiet as we watched the ambulance taking his son to hospital pull away and heard the wail of its siren.

Then it was interviews, solicitors, statements, the whole deal. I was in trouble for having an unlicensed pistol and allowing it to be used in a killing. Hank was in trouble over the stun gun. We were all culpable for failing to report a kidnapping and sundry other offences. Near the end of it all I was wrung out and short-tempered and my solicitor, Viv Garner, had to advise me to calm down. We had the chance for a quiet talk during one of the breaks in the interrogation and recording process.

'It'll sort out, Cliff,' he said. 'Another suspension most likely, at worst.'

My throat was dry from lousy coffee and talking. I shook my head. 'Not this time. I've had too many of them. The police'll recommend to the board to lift it permanently.'

'We'll see. Just play along. Don't give them any more to work with. Is there any more? What am I saying? With you, there's always more.'

'I called Rex Wain's killing in anonymously.'

'Just keep quiet about that.'

'I'm worried about Hank. He could be deported. I wonder what Frank's saying?'

'Worry about yourself, mate.'

*

The wash-up could have been worse. The coroner found that Sawtell's death was the result of a justifiable homicide. The police had pushed hard for this, not only because of Frank's exemplary record, but because they were happy to have Wain's murder cleared up—ballistics showed that Sawtell's pistol had done the job—and to have Sawtell himself off their books. It didn't take too much cynicism to understand that the police were happy to have him silenced forever, unable to name names.

With this background they came down lighter on Hank, who incurred a year's suspension of his PEA licence and a period of community service.

'He's an American,' Viv Garner said. 'We don't deport Americans or give them a hard time. Softly, softly.'

I was charged with a firearms offence, conspiracy to conceal a crime and violation of an earlier adverse order governing my conduct as a private enquiry agent. I was given a suspended gaol sentence. My licence was cancelled with a rider that I was ineligible to apply for it to be restored.

'That's unconstitutional,' Viv Garner said. 'We'll appeal.'

I shrugged. 'Let's talk about it.'

William Heysen recovered from his wound, probably thanks to Frank's intervention, because Sawtell's bullet had nicked an artery. Frank visited him in hospital a few times but they didn't hit it off.

'He was humiliated by being taken in by Sawtell,' Frank said. 'Thought he was smarter than that.'

'He should be grateful to you for saving his life.'

'He doesn't think of it like that. I don't know how he

thinks. Then there's all this stuff about Heysen and his mother and Sawtell and me and others. He's carrying a lot of baggage. He's hard to reach.'

'He might improve.'

'He might get worse. Would you believe? He knows all about this DNA testing. He says it can only prove that a man can't be the father of a particular person, not that someone else definitely is. There's only a ninety-five point five per cent likelihood. He reckons he'll go with the four point five per cent.'

I could tell that this hurt him deeply but on balance I thought he'd be better off with things arranged that way.

'Forget him,' I said. 'You've got Peter.'

Peter Parker and Ramona had two healthy daughters and took off for Africa with them when the children were six weeks old. Frank and Hilde made plans to visit them. Frank was out of the undertow.

An earthquake hit Indonesia and created havoc where the tsunami had already killed hundreds of people and flattened everything in sight. An Australian relief helicopter crashed and nine service people were killed. It was a boom time for tabloid newspapers and television. The pope died and Charles and Camilla got married, two events I tried to ignore.

Lily and I went on as before, coming and going. We took Ruby Gentle for dinner at the Bourbon and Beefsteak and she demolished her two-person chateaubriand with ease. We had a great night, but Lily passed on the biography.

The appeal mounted by Viv Garner and supported by Frank Parker and others' testimonials to my sterling character failed. As Detective Sergeant Carr had said, I was carrying too much maverick baggage and the licensing board was happy to make an example of me. The profession in future was to be conducted differently.

I couldn't work and the bills kept coming. I ran short of money and made an unannounced visit to Catherine Heysen, who had set the whole thing in motion, to present my unpaid account. She was living in a luxury unit in Potts Point, the Earlwood house having sold for a bundle.

When I identified myself I could hear hesitation before she admitted me. She'd completely recovered from her injury and was her old, cold, composed, regal self in a blue dress, perfect makeup and surroundings to match.

'I'm sorry, Mr Hardy,' she said after I'd given her the itemised account, 'I've neglected you.'

'A cheque will repair my damaged feelings.'

'You don't like me.'

'I never did. It doesn't matter.'

She chewed that over, decided not to work against it, and wrote me a cheque for the amount outstanding.

'William and I are reconciled,' she said.

'That's nice. Pity he didn't thank Frank for saving his life.'

'He says it was a slight wound, scarcely worse than mine.'

I laughed. I could imagine William saying just that. He'd tell her whatever he thought she'd want to hear for just as long as it suited him. And no longer.

'You don't like him either.'

'Neither does his probable father.'

'That's a pity. As I say, we're close again. William didn't commit any crimes in his association with Matthew Sawtell.'

'Not that anyone could prove. He came close, probably did.'

'He lost money, of course, but I have plenty as you can see.' She waved her hand at the furniture and fittings. 'We're going into the fashion business together. With my contacts and William's charm and language skills, I'm sure we will be successful.'

'Good luck,' I said, but I didn't mean it, though it would be interesting to see which one of them came out on top.